Mythical Girls

Celticfrog Publishing.

Alex McGilvery
Editor

Honourary Editors
David Goodwin
Peggy McAloon
Macartney Halls

Authors

Abiran Raveenthiran
Alex McGilvery
Blazej Szpakowicz
Byrne Montgomery
Deanna Baran
Eileen Bell
Jacob Rundle
James Ricket
Jessica Renwick
Kandi J. Wyatt
Miriam Rainbird

Illustrator

Lucy Harnett

Lucy was born in Kamloops, BC and now resides in the lower mainland with her brother, father and is surrounded by her immediate family. Lucy started drawing at the age of 9 after being inspired by a series called *Fullmetal Alchemist*. She immediately began putting in long hours and working hard to perfect her craft. She has aspirations of being a professional manga artist, residing in Japan and one day having her own manga publication.

Front Cover

The photographer for the front cover is AMAImagery.
The model if Kell-c Jules

Mythical Girls

ISBN 978-1-989092-37-8

Abiran Raveenthiran is a first-generation born Canadian as many are in the cultural melting pot that is Toronto, Ontario. He has one foot in the culture of his past and one foot in the present culture with views into both. His works are written in a way to merge concepts of the eastern and western culture together; a product mirroring his own identity. Abiran has previously published works of non-fiction essays through The Lemon Theory and TamilCulture. He has more stories being released in the same universe as Daybreak coming soon. For more information please follow him on Instagram @lightweaversreads.

Daybreak

By Abiran Raveenthiran

Rajakumari peered out the window and wondered which member of her family would try to kill her this time. Dark, the sky let tears fall to the earth. Every so often, it screamed and shouted as the lightning parted the clouds. Even the sky mourned the death of King Chayaan—undoubtedly, the greatest king to ever live. The only things louder than the wails of the sky were the wails of Queen Lakshmi in the nursery.

Near the edge of the window was a double-headed cobra-a rare species. It coiled its body around three newly hatched babes, allowing both hoods of the neck to shelter them from the pelting rain.

This night, Queen Lakshmi was experiencing the joys and pains of bringing a child into this world. A scream louder than Rajakumari had expected caught her by surprise. A servant ran to Rajakumari with a bundle of sheets wrapped in her hands. The woman handed Rajakumari the bundle. In it was a male babe, fresh and crying.

"King Chayaan has returned to us," the servant said with tears in her eyes. "The God King has returned to us once more."

Rajakumari looked at the babe. It would take but a second for her to crush his fragile neck. She could end a war over the claim to the throne in a single, sinful act. Her own son or Queen Lakshmi's. The firstborn son or the son born of the first wife. Her love for King Chayaan suddenly evolved into resentment. If he hadn't taken on three wives, this decision would never have come to be. Even more, she resented him for not being alive. This decision would never have been needed if he was. Tears fell from her face. One act that she would regret for the rest of her life. The death of a single, innocent child was all it would take to avoid conflict.

Suddenly, she was aware of her quivering hand slowly approaching the babe. Her eyes moved from his neck to his face. Then, she saw what the wet nurse had meant. His eyes had the same fiery red tinge as King Chayaan; his nose, the same slender curve; his giggle, the same pitch. Steadying her hand, she lightly touched the side of the babe's face.

Rajakumari looked up, realizing the wet nurse had more to say, and nodded for her to continue. But a tug of her finger caught her attention once more. The newborn's strength was astounding for a babe.

"The reincarnation of King Chayaan himself," she whispered, kissing him on his forehead.

"As the sun rises, the moon sets," said the wet nurse. "For King Chayaan to return to us once more, Queen Lakshmi has... set." Set. It was the same word they had used when King Chayaan had passed away. *His time had set. His rein had set. The sun now sets on the Thambiah Kingdom.*

General Kattappan appeared beside her. His beard was thick and curled inward. He wore the sun emblem of the Thambiah Kingdom proudly on his chest. Even in these dark days, his loyalty and prideful posture somehow made the sun emblem shine bright. If she had known his thoughts, he surely would have killed her. The ends of her lips curled in an all-knowing smile. There was solace in knowing that loyalty ran in his veins instead of blood. And that loyalty would guarantee the well-being of the kingdom.

"Queen Rajakumari, the Nobles of the houses have called an emergency meeting. It may have been caused by the siege by Queen Asurani. Her people are few in numbers but appear to have strength in strategy. Fortunately, we have been able to barely keep them at bay. If the kingdom had maintained a united front, the battle might have gone differently. As the royalty of the kingdom is torn, so are the armies. We have been divided, and now many support the false queen." Kattappan said with his head bowed. Asurani, the third wife of King Chayaan, had fled to her native kingdom even before the death. Many suspected the death had been caused by his last wife, Asurani.

The emergency meeting should have been for the first wife of King Chayaan to resolve. Now, it was Rajakumari's right to take charge.

"There is another issue." General Kattappan's voice was grim.

"What is it?"

"The sword, my queen. Queen Asurani carries *his* sword. You know as well as I the power it wields." That she did. Daybreak, the sword of her late husband, was magnificent to lay one's eyes upon and even more so to wield. It appeared to be made of countless red and orange shards, intricately placed together. Separately, the shards had no power, but together they were enough to break down the walls of the kingdom. Now that it was known that Asurani wielded the legendary sword, time was running out.

"Let us see to them. Prepare the Meeting Room for my entry," Rajakumari ordered.

As Kattappan was about to leave, she grabbed his hand. The soldier, eyes brimming with ages of war and wisdom far beyond his years, looked back. "Remember, Kattappan. The sun will rise again."

He nodded. The words did not evoke the same emotion as when her late husband had said them. They were the motto of the kingdom to give an inspiring light in dark days. Then again, these days were worse than dark. These days were midnight black. These days even the faintest candlelight shone bright in the darkest room.

***

Rajakumari strode into the throne room with her babe in one hand and Lakshmi's in the other. Her sari flowed behind her. The noblemen lined up near the entrance with a troop of soldiers behind. She instinctively walked to the throne to the left of the King's but stopped herself. The first wife was dead—meaning that the seat was now Rajakumari's. She walked to the throne to the right of the king's own. She sat in it, and somehow felt it that it had always been hers.

She sat differently in this one, her right leg on the seat with her. In her left arm, her own babe, Bhallal, lay quietly, while supported by her right leg and part of her body was Lakshmi's babe, whom she would name Bali. The seating arrangement allowed her to the use one hand as she spoke.

"Why have you called this meeting? This is not the right time for it. It is the middle of the night, and a storm wakes in our palace." Rajakumari spoke with deliberate intensity.

"This is a matter of urgency." A nobleman, Chandran, stepped forward. "We need to know who is now in charge of matters. King Chayaan has fallen. There are wars waging; one at our own doorstep. The kingdom needs leadership."

"This is true. That is why I appoint myself to lead this kingdom." Another nobleman, Senju, stepped forward. To Rajakumari's knowledge, he'd had his eye on the throne for quite some time but had never known how to place himself there. Like a snake, he slithered his way in.

"That is preposterous. The king's brother, Bijjal, still lives. Cripple he may be, but his mind is still of use," another nobleman replied.

"What of Queen Asurani? She has already proven to be worthy to command an army of her own," another jested to which the men laughed, as though a woman could not command these lands as well as a man.

The noblemen continued to argue. Some acted as though the throne was already theirs. Others supported the noblemen they wished to claim the throne for their own agenda. They had all forgotten the queen in their midst.

"Silence!" Rajakumari shouted. Her voice echoed in the large room, surprising her as well as the noblemen. It sounded elegant, intimidating, and inspiring—just like her late husband's. Perhaps it was the throne doing the talking. "What of the babes of the King? It must be they who rule."

"Have you gone mad, woman?" Senju asked. "They are babes. We are in the middle of a war, and one we may not win. There are reports she carries Daybreak. The kingdom needs leadership. Who will lead the kingdom until they are of age? There are two equal claims to the throne. Even if we were to let them grow to see better days, who would rule? There can only be one king."

Rajakumari sat with her chest out, an air of confidence surrounding her. Senju's eyes widened.

"You? You cannot be serious. We cannot have a woman lead the kingdom. War is not the same as preparing a hot chicken curry in the kitchen. There are lives at stake," Senju said.

"There are lives at stake in the kitchen too—the chickens'," another nobleman laughed.

"You insult your queen? The two children have an equal right to the throne. One is the firstborn to King Chayaan, while the other is the first son of the first wife of the king. They will compete for the throne when they

are of age. I will watch the kingdom until then." Senju opened his mouth, but Rajakumari cut him off with a wave of her hand. "King Chayaan's era has set. Queen Lakshmi has fallen. All that remains is my word. And my word is now law. Whoever supports my cause, step to the right. The others go to the left."

Three noblemen made their way to the right side of the room. The others placed themselves on the left. The three were an older bunch and had been extremely loyal to King Chayaan. She had known the outcome before it occurred. Still, she gave them the benefit of the doubt.

"And that is your final decision?" she asked. The noblemen remained in silent agreement.

"So be it. Kattappan, clean the filth from our midst! These men intend to tarnish the Thambiah Kingdom," Rajakumari shouted, pointing at the left-hand group. On cue, Kattappan ran into the room with his sword unsheathed.

"What is going on?" One of the noblemen shuddered and slid deeper into the crowd.

"Purification," Rajakumari whispered to the babes in her hands.

Kattappan ran and hacked away at the men. Some attempted to fight back, but none were as skilled as Kattappan—the whole kingdom knew that to be true.

Rajakumari saw Senju retreat to the troops in the back. "Kill Kattappan and Rajakumari," he said, pointing at the two.

The troops marched forward. They may have looked proud, marching with the sun emblem, but she only saw traitors. Traitors who needed to be slaughtered. They marched forward in unison. There was a reason she had only brought one soldier. It was because there was only one she needed. He ran toward them and with prowess slew man after man, soldier after soldier, life after life. He may have been the embodiment of loyalty, but the man was also the embodiment of war. None could stand up to a man such as him. He wielded the sword as though he had been born with it.

One of the noblemen escaped Kattappan's purification and ran toward her with his sword out.

"On whatever honour I might have left, I swear I will end you for what you've done," the nobleman spat. Rajakumari had never met this man. Neither would she get the chance to know him. With her free hand, she threw a dagger that landed in the center of the nobleman's face. He died before his body even hit the ground. Whatever sense of twisted honour he had died with him.

They often forgot who Rajakumari was. Each queen had a skill of her own. Queen Lakshmi, her gift in dancing; Asurani, in music and poems. But Rajakumari was nothing like them. Her prowess was in the art of fighting.

She had concentrated solely on her own opponent and not on Kattappan. She now realized that he had become outnumbered while her attention was elsewhere. The soldiers held a sword to his neck. "Traitors," she spat.

"Yield," the solder declared. The proud soldier who had fought valiantly against them only gritted his teeth and attempted to struggle his way out. Blood poured from a fresh wound near his arm.

One of the soldiers walked up to her, the sun emblem on his chest splattered with blood. Rajakumari's grip tightened on her dagger. She was ready to pounce like a tigress of the jungle. Little did the soldier know of her savagery. He would suffer for it.

"You may kill me. Maybe the next soldier who comes. Or the one after that. But even you can only fight so many of us. Give up now and surrender. If not for you, then for the lives of the princes. We do not wish to kill them any more than you.

Still, we will do it if it is necessary. Yield. And tell your dog to do the same."

Rajakumari met his eyes. There was truth in them. Saddened truth. Her hand relaxed on the dagger. There were more lives at stake than just her own. The children in her hands would not even have the chance to reign if she blundered. She waved with one hand to signal Kattappan to relax. There had to be another way to get out of this situation.

Tremors shook the ground, subtle but undeniable. The sound of clanking metal entered the room. Everyone looked from door to door to see where it was coming from, but the metallic sound echoed in the large hall. All the doors opened at once and in came soldiers marching in unison, filling the room. They wore emblems of an owl, unlike the Thambiah Kingdom's sun emblem. Some of them turned and made a pathway through. A woman in an elegant blue sari entered through it.

She walked past the soldier and with a simple push moved him out of her way. She knelt before Rajakumari.

"Asurani?" the queen asked, confused.

"Yes. I have been trying to come to warn you of the conspiracy in this kingdom. Your soldiers would hear none of it and assumed it was some plan to overthrow you and Lakshmi. I want no such thing. The crown has killed the one man I loved. I hate it, but I cannot take the right to it away from my child." Rajakumari looked at her sister through marriage. She had never known Asurani was with child. The woman snapped her fingers, and a soldier appeared with a ball of silk and cotton. In it was a babe only a few weeks born.

"What do you want of me?" Rajakumari asked.

"I overheard your meeting with the noblemen. All I wish is for my son to be granted the same chance as the two babes in your hands. Isn't he as much your son as they?" Asurani looked up at Rajakumari. "I want none of this. The royalty. The crown. They can have it all. Until they can, you can have it all. I only wish to witness my child grow. Let the loyalty of these soldiers be my gift to you in efforts of forging this new alliance, my queen."

Rajakumari nodded and accepted the gift. The soldier placed the child near her thigh. She looked from one babe to the next. They were all different in their own ways but shared something common. They all had features of her late husband. One, his eyes; the second, his nose; and the third, his mouth. Rajakumari saw the future and past of the kingdom, in the present moment.

Bali began to cry. Rajakumari lifted her three children, two in one arm and one in the other. The storm had stopped, and a few cracks of the sun rays penetrated the clouds.

"You made Bali cry with your words," Rajakumari said.

Asurani tensed. She was ready to move quickly, if need be. There was fear and caution in her. Rajakumari saw it now, the blade of a warrior was partially hidden in her blue sari, the red and orange shards radiantly shining through. Daybreak was among them.

Rajakumari continued. "Dark days and dark times caused mistrust within the kingdom. We must look past that. The sun must rise again. As it rises, let these dark shadows slither and hide from us. We are Queens of the Sun. Not just me and not just you. Together we must rule until our sons can."

"I would be honoured," Asurani said as she extended the shard sword, hilt first.

"What of this?"

"I will assist as best as I can, but the hilt only has space for one hand. It must be yours." Rajakumari took the sword in one hand. Rays of sunlight came through the room and parted through Daybreak, dazzling everyone in the room, including Rajakumari. What dazzled more in Rajakumari's eyes was her sister's words.

Her inspiring speech had inspired one of the children to leave a strong-scented present.

"After all, I am going to need help to raise kings," Rajakumari said. She handed over Bali to Asurani, assuming he was the one who had left the present.

Asurani smiled. It washed over Rajakumari like the warm rays of the sun's radiance. She reached into her blue sari and pulled out a wooden flute. "Sorry, sister. This moment calls for music. It will have to be you to change them. I'll do what I am best at, and you do what you are best at."

Rajakumari raised her eyebrow. "Cleaning baby bottoms?"

Asurani shrugged. "Purify them too," she laughed. As the sun washed over the land, Asurani played an aubade welcoming its presence.

Rajakumari waved her hand. The new, loyal soldiers continued the job Kattappan had started. They were swift and efficient. The noblemen and traitorous soldiers had no chance of escape.

"Hold them for a second," Rajakumari said, handing one child at a time to Asurani and the nearby wet nurse.

"What is it, your highness?"

"Let me test the sword that will go to one of our sons." So Rajakumari unleashed fury upon the remaining traitors like no one had ever seen. The new soldiers stepped back and watched as she quenched the sword's bloodlust. As light entered the shards of Daybreak, it reflected, leaving an orange glow.

"Blue to blend into the sky,
Green to forge anew for the present,

Red to remember what was once forgotten or yet to be forgotten."

Rajakumari had known these words about the shards since childhood. There were more, but they slipped her mind. *Orange. What was orange?*

Asurani stopped playing music and smiled. "Orange to protect what is worth protecting."

"The kingdom," Rajakumari said. "That is what is worth protecting."

Asurani turned so that the children were visible. "That and the children. The children are what is worth protecting."

Rajakumari nodded in agreement.

"Was this what you wanted? You were always one that I could never understand. You were just born too ahead of your time for us to catch up," Rajakumari said, looking into the eyes of one child, the nose of another and the mouth of the last.

That was the point in history that led to the rebirth of the Thambiah Kingdom. As the sun rose in the air, the kingdom had indirectly appointed two queens. And the queens would rule in unison, one with an iron fist and the other with an iron heart. With the rising sun, there was now a purity in the kingdom. No more broken alliances and feuding families. All of this would change—had changed—with the double reigning queens.

James Rickett lives in Texarkana, Texas with his wife Catherine and their three children. He develops computer software for a living, and in his spare time he enjoys writing, piano, drawing, cooking, and video games. His favorite writers are C. S. Lewis, J. R. R. Tolkien, and G. K. Chesterton. He is currently working on his first novel.

Skyvale

By James Rickett

"Ugh! I can't believe we have to go pick stupid mushrooms again." Lindy trudged along the wooded path to the Grove. It was a warm spring day, and beams of sunlight shone through the branches of the oaks and spruces around them.

"But it's one of our main sources of food and Skyvale's biggest export to the outside world." Miki walked beside her.

"But I hate mushrooms. They're so gross and rubbery." Lindy started the descent into the grove, a cool, damp tract of land between two huge overhanging cliff faces. Mushrooms of all sizes and shapes grew there.

"I know. You've told me a hundred times," Miki said. "But everyone else in the village likes them."

"Then everyone else in the village can go pick them." A light breeze carried an earthy fungus smell with it. Lindy wrinkled her nose and brushed her grass-green hair out of her round face.

"We all have our jobs to do," Miki said. They walked through a thicket of plump oakwood mushrooms taller than themselves.

"Yeah, I know," Lindy muttered. "I wish there was some way to get off this island. Then maybe I could do something besides mushroom farming."

"Nobody's forcing you to stay," Miki said. "Remember Haslett? Didn't he hitch a ride on one of the merchant airships and move to Dulain?"

"Yeah, but he was of age when he left. We're only fifteen."

"So you'll just have to wait three more years."

"That seems like forever." Lindy stepped around a large patch of morels.

"What would you do, anyway?" Miki asked.

"I don't know. Something big. Do you know what Haslett is doing now?"

"I heard he ended up joining a pirate airship."

"Oh," Lindy said. "Well, of course I wouldn't be a pirate."

"I sure hope not," Miki said. "I hope you don't leave at all. Anyway, I've heard the sky pirates have been seen more often. We might not be as safe here as the elders have always thought. The traders on the supply airship told my parents they've already attacked at least two sky settlements in the past year."

"What? Why haven't I heard about this?" Lindy scanned the horizon, afraid she would see a marauding pirate ship already on its way.

"I just found out myself," Miki said. "I think the elders are trying to keep quiet about it so people don't panic. It's only a matter of time before everybody finds out though."

They went to their favorite spot, which they reached by going through a narrow crevice in one of the cliffs, hidden behind some bushes. Miki insisted they avoid being seen by the other mushroom pickers. Gas plants grew in the passage, and they had to be careful to avoid popping them.

"Tell me again why we have to go through this tiny hole." Lindy struggled to squeeze through a tight space between two large slabs of rock, feeling slightly annoyed that Miki's taller, slimmer figure allowed her to get through it easier.

"Because the best mushrooms grow here, and nobody else knows about it." Miki gently shoved aside a floating gas plant. "And try to be quiet; I'd like to keep this place a secret."

They entered a spacious area enclosed by high rock walls. A faint beam of sunlight shone down in the centre, and several orange butterflies flitted about. They slipped their baskets off their backs. Miki tied her long pink hair behind her head with a ribbon while Lindy stood with her shoulders slumped and surveyed the endless expanse of mushrooms.

"Lindy, there are better ones over here." Miki beckoned from where she stood next to a cluster of tree-sized mushrooms.

"Great," Lindy said. "Maybe they'll be delicious enough that I'll actually be able to choke one down without gagging."

As Lindy got down on her knees, she saw a glint on the ground from a ray of sunlight. Something metallic protruded from the earth next to one of the giant mushrooms. Excited by the chance to do something besides picking mushrooms, she started brushing away the loose topsoil around it.

"What's that?" Miki said.

"Something's buried here." Lindy felt the edges of the object. "I think it's a box."

"Dig it out," Miki said. "Let's find out what's in it!"

Lindy grabbed one of the edges while Miki knelt down and pulled on another edge. They extracted a small iron box. Lindy picked it up and brushed off the dirt, revealing a glyph shaped like a tree with a bee above it. Below was the letter *H*.

"Miki, look, this is my family crest! This *H* must be for my last name. This box must have belonged to one of my ancestors."

"So what's in it?" Miki snatched the box away from Lindy and tried to pry the lid off.

"Let me try; I'm stronger." Lindy grabbed the box and pulled.

"I've almost got it!" Miki scowled and gripped her side of the box tighter.

The girls tugged at the box until the lid popped off, and then they both fell on their backs. Lindy's head smashed into a large overripe mushroom. Something round and silvery flew out

of the box, glinted in the sunlight, and landed a few feet away. They both scrambled toward it, and Lindy reached it first.

It was a simple, silver bracelet. Lindy picked it up and examined it. It felt strangely warm and gave off a curious energy.

"It's pretty," Miki said. "And so shiny."

“Yeah, it’s not tarnished at all,” Lindy said. “And it feels weird. I wonder if...”

“Do you think it might be magical?” Miki whispered.

“If it is, I wonder what it does.”

“Who cares? You know magical relics aren’t allowed in Skyvale. They haven’t been allowed since our ancestors came here from the Lands Below.”

“That’s a stupid rule,” Lindy said. “People are so closed-minded here! I say we keep it. It probably belongs to my family by rights, anyway. Maybe it was even used by one of the old Guardians.”

“I just don’t want you to get in trouble,” Miki said. “I think you should put it back.”

“What’s the worst that could happen? They’d just take it away. But I wonder why somebody didn’t do a better job of hiding it? It was hardly even covered up.”

“My guess is it was buried deeper.” Miki stood up and put her hand on the giant mushroom. “But this mushroom tree started growing in the same place and forced it up to the surface. It must have been buried by one of the original founders of Skyvale, like your great-great-grandfather or something, when they outlawed magical relics.”

“I guess he couldn’t bear to destroy it, so he hid it instead.” Lindy gazed at the clouds overhead. “I wonder if he’s looking down from the Upper Skies right now, happy that his great-great-granddaughter was the one to find it. I wonder if he was a Guardian?”

Lindy put her fingers through the bracelet. It looked too small to fit around her wrist, let alone get her whole hand through it, but as she pushed it toward her knuckles, it started expanding.

“Look at that!” Lindy said. “It’s getting bigger.”

Miki's eyes widened. "It's definitely magical then."

Lindy slipped her hand through it, and it shrank again until it was snug on her wrist.

"So what does it do?" Miki said.

"How should I know?" Lindy waved her arm up and down. "Maybe it has the power to pick mushrooms for me." She concentrated on the bracelet, and her feet lifted slightly off the ground. It was like floating in water, but lighter and freer.

Miki shrieked. "Lindy, you're flying! Or am I seeing things?" She rubbed her eyes. "Have we been picking the wrong kind of mushroom?"

Lindy willed herself to stop hovering and immediately dropped back to the ground.

"That was fun!" Lindy made herself float again. This time, she levitated several feet.

"Be careful!" Miki looked up, pressing her hands together and grimacing.

Lindy lost her balance, wobbled around, and fell sprawling into a patch of puffballs, sending a cloud of spores into the air.

"Are you okay?" Miki held out her hand to help Lindy up.

Lindy climbed to her feet, coughing. "This is great! Do you want to try it?"

"I don't think so. You know how scared of heights I am. You keep it. Maybe you can use it to... I don't know, save the village, or something."

"Me, save the village? From what?" Lindy laughed. "I think I'll just go home and take a bath instead." She pulled off the bracelet and stuck it in her shorts pocket.

After finishing their harvest, the girls picked up their baskets and made their way back through the crevice. As they walked through the Grove, Lindy noticed three older teenage boys surrounding a smaller boy with a basket of mushrooms on his back.

"Look, it's Rynden and his goons," Miki whispered.

"I see you've brought me some mushrooms, Marden." Rynden sneered. He wore a fancy embroidered tunic over his shirt that matched his curly maroon hair.

"But… these are mine," Marden said in a rather squeaky voice.

"Correction: they were yours," Rynden said. His companions grinned at each other.

"It must be nice to be a village elder's son," Lindy muttered. "You get to extort people all you want, and nobody does anything about it."

Marden slowly pulled the basket off his back and handed it to one of Rynden's companions.

"I'll even do you a favour, because I'm a nice guy," Rynden said. He took Marden's basket, emptied its contents into his own, and handed it back to Marden.

"Here, now at least you still have a basket," Rynden said. "Thanks for your service."

"It's so unfair." Lindy gripped the straps of her own basket.

"I know, but what can we do?" Miki said. "Let's just go before they notice us."

"If he tries to take my stuff, I'll fight him," Lindy said. "I'll throw a mushroom in his face."

"I don't think we have to worry; he usually doesn't pick on girls," Miki said. "At least not in the same way."

Another young man approached. He had dark blue-green hair and he carried a wide, flat handbasket. "Hey, Rynden, how's the stealing going? Must be hard work."

"Mind your own business, Garrett," Rynden said.

"Maybe you should mind your own business too, and stop taking other people's stuff." Garrett faced Rynden and his two companions, his expression calm. Garrett and Rynden were of equal stature, but Rynden's goons were noticeably bulkier.

Lindy and Miki exchanged glances. "He's so brave," Lindy whispered. "We should go help him out." She started to walk toward them.

"It's okay," Marden said. "I… I don't mind doing my part to support the village."

"See, Marden knows his place." Rynden crossed his arms. "You should learn from his example."

"Whatever," Garrett muttered. He shook his head and walked away from them. Rynden's companions laughed and started off in the opposite direction.

Garrett's eyes met Lindy's as she walked toward him.

"Um, hi, Lindy." He smiled nervously.

"Hi," Lindy said. "I was coming to help you deal with Rynden and his pals, but I guess I'm too late, right?"

"Better late than never," Garrett said. "How's the mushroom picking? It looks like you had a rough time."

Lindy remembered she was still covered in spore dust and mushroom bits. "Oh, just a typical day at the Grove for me."

"Well, you still look pretty… nice." Garrett's face reddened.

"Garrett!" an older woman's voice called out.

"That's my grandmother." Garrett frowned. "I have to go help her harvest velvet stems." He held up his basket. "I guess I'll see you later." He turned and walked away.

Miki walked up to where Lindy was standing. "So, how did it go?"

"Uh, good, I think." Lindy picked a piece of mushroom out of her hair. "He sort of said I looked pretty."

"Well, that's sort of a good sign," Miki said. "Hey, let's go help Marden refill his mushroom basket."

"Good idea," Lindy said.

* * *

Later that afternoon, Lindy sneaked out of the house, making sure the bracelet was still in her pocket. Taking the trail to the Dropoff, she went only halfway there and then entered the woods. She looked around to make sure nobody was there, and then put the bracelet on her wrist and practised using its powers. The weightless feeling in her limbs was exhilarating.

She drifted up until she was floating over the tops of the trees. From this vantage point, she could see the edge of the sky island and the dim, foggy shapes of mountains and valleys far below. She wanted to go higher, but she was afraid she might be seen from the village. After amusing herself for a while, she floated back to the ground, slipped off the bracelet, and returned home.

This became a routine over the next couple of days. Lindy discovered she had sharper senses and greater strength while wearing the bracelet. She tested this by lifting a large rock she would never have been able to pick up without the bracelet. Her daydreams about leaving Skyvale became more frequent. She had real power now; she could do whatever she wanted.

But that's a dumb idea, she thought. *My family and friends are here. Garrett is here. Out in the wide world, I have nobody.* Nevertheless, she couldn't help but be curious about what was out there. She thought about going to the Dropoff and floating all the way down to the Lands Below, but couldn't work up the courage, terrified both of flying that far down and of who or what she might meet down there.

As she walked down the path from the village square to her house, she ran into Miki.

"Hey, Lindy, do you want to pick mushrooms with me tomorrow morning?"

"I'm sorry, but I have some other chores to do then." The lie caused a twinge of guilt. *Why do I feel like I'm too good to pick mushrooms now? Well, once the novelty of having this bracelet wears off, I'll go back to spending more time with Miki.*

"You've been avoiding everyone," Miki said.

Lindy looked down at her own feet.

"It's that bracelet, isn't it?" Miki sighed. "You've been going out alone to use it."

"Just a tiny bit. I'm practising in case I have to... save the village, or something." Lindy laughed a little at her feeble joke.

"It's okay; I won't tell anyone. Well, I guess I'll see you later." Miki walked away before Lindy could figure out how to apologize to her.

When she got to her house, her brother, Ashton, was standing at the front door, holding a slingshot in his hand. He had grass-green hair like Lindy.

"Watch this, Lindy," Ashton said.

He aimed his slingshot at a floating gas plant, pulled back, and fired. The stone hit the plant's air sack and punctured it with a loud pop. The entire plant flew back as the escaping air propelled it away from them.

"Isn't that awesome?" Ashton laughed.

"Yeah, that's great, Ashton." Lindy walked past him. "I did the same thing a million times when I was your age."

"Lindy, you promised me you'd take me to the Silver Falls when you got home." Ashton crossed his arms.

"Not now, I'm busy."

"Busy doing what? Mother says you've been skipping your chores."

"Maybe I'm just skipping the unimportant chores because I have more important chores to do!" Lindy walked across the wooden planks of the front porch.

"That doesn't make any sense. Wait, Lindy, you promised!"

Lindy ignored Ashton and went into the house. The floor and walls were constructed of light wood panels. The brightly coloured rugs on the floor and glow-lamps hanging on the walls gave the interior a cheery atmosphere. Lindy went straight to her bedroom, where she spent the next hour practising with the bracelet.

* * *

"Lindy!" Mother called. Lindy slipped off the bracelet and walked into the kitchen, where Mother was putting groceries away.

"Where's Ashton?" Mother said. "And where have you been all day?"

"Nowhere," Lindy said. "Just walking around."

"By yourself?" Mother put a package of meat into the cold storage box.

"Yeah, why not?"

"There's nothing wrong with it. It just doesn't seem like you." Mother sat down in a chair.

"Maybe I like the peace and quiet."

"Lindy, what's wrong? You haven't been keeping up with your chores, and you haven't been treating your brother very nicely, either."

Someone knocked on the door. Lindy walked over and opened it, relieved she didn't have to deal with the question. Garrett stood at the entrance.

"Um, hi, Lindy." He glanced quickly around the room.

"Hi, Garrett." Lindy felt her stomach flutter. "Would you like to come in?"

"Thank you." Garrett stepped inside.

Lindy noticed a dagger in a shiny sheath on Garrett's belt. "Is that a new dagger?"

"Yeah, I bought it from the supply airship last time it came." He turned to Lindy's mother. "Mrs. Honeytree, I think Ashton might be at the Dropoff with some friends."

"What? Why?" Mother stood up quickly.

"I think they're playing a game where they dare each other to get as close to the edge as possible," Garrett said.

"Those stupid boys!" Mother paced across the room. "I've told the elders we should be posting a guard there. We need to go find them, right now."

"I can help." Garrett glanced at Lindy. She beamed at him.

"Thank you, Garrett," Mother said. "Lindy, you and Garrett go ahead to the Dropoff while I go find your father."

"We'll do it," Garrett said.

Once they were outside, Lindy's mother strode in the direction of the village square. Lindy's hands trembled. She wasn't sure how much of it was fear about her brother's safety and how much was excitement about being with Garrett. Her hand went to her pocket and closed around the bracelet.

"I meant to tell you, I thought you were very brave, standing up to Rynden at the Grove," Lindy said as they jogged down the path to the Dropoff.

"Really?" Garrett said. "Thanks. Not that it did much good, though."

"I'm glad you tried," Lindy said. "It's not fair that he keeps getting away with that."

"Well, life isn't exactly fair."

"I know, but if more people could just stand up and do what's right... I wish I could do that."

"I think you could, Lindy."

After hearing him say her name, Lindy almost blurted out her feelings for him, but she pressed her lips together to stop herself. *Probably not a good idea at the moment, anyway.*

"So, have you ever felt like... leaving Skyvale?" Lindy asked.

"A couple of times. You don't want to leave, do you?"

Does that mean he wants me to stay? "I don't know. I just feel like this place is too small."

"Maybe, but it's peaceful here, and most people take care of each other—aside from the occasional jerk."

He's right, you know. "What if you had the power to do something about the occasional jerk?"

"You mean, like, if I was an elder?"

"No, I was thinking real power."

"Like having an ancient relic?"

Should I tell him? "Yeah, something like that."

"Well, I don't know if I'd trust myself with something like that," Garrett said. "But since they're all lost now, I guess it doesn't matter. Besides, there's other ways to deal with problems like that."

Maybe he should have it instead. Lindy started getting short of breath, so she stopped talking.

"Are you okay?" Garrett said. "We can slow down if you want."

"I'm fine." *Can't have him thinking I'm weak.*

A couple minutes later, they reached the end of the woods, with the Dropoff just beyond. Lindy's heart raced from the exertion, and Garrett was taking deep breaths. It looked like they were at the top of a massive cliff, but this was actually the edge of the great sky island they lived on. The Lands Below were a vast expanse of mountains, forests, plains, and rivers. Several boys and girls nearby laughed and yelled.

"It looks like we got here just in time," Garrett said. "Everyone, get away from the edge!"

Most of the kids obeyed, but to Lindy's dismay, Rynden stood at the edge with his two friends, taunting some younger boys. He held a boy with grass-green hair by the front of his shirt, pushing him toward the very edge of the Dropoff. Lindy's stomach sank as she and Garrett hurried toward them.

"Lindy, help me!" Ashton said.

Rynden turned around, still holding Ashton by his shirt, and looked at Garrett. "Well, if it isn't the Guardian of Skyvale."

"You know it's forbidden to be at the Dropoff," Garrett said.

"You're not in charge here," Rynden said. "Besides, we're just having a little fun, aren't we? I'm teaching these kids how to conquer their fears."

Garrett took a step forward. "The lesson's over."

"Rynden, please let my brother go," Lindy pleaded.

Rynden hesitated, then slowly relaxed his grip on Ashton's shirt.

One of Rynden's lackeys snarled, "We'll teach you to respect your betters." He swung his fist at Garrett.

Garrett blocked it and shoved him back, causing him to bump into Ashton. Ashton lost his balance and fell backward off the edge of the Dropoff.

"Ashton!" Lindy screamed.

"Help!" Ashton called out from below.

Everyone rushed to the edge and gaped. Ashton clung to an outcropping with both hands. Rynden and his friends stared in horror.

"I'm going down there." Garrett got on his hands and knees and prepared to climb down.

But the cliff face was too sheer, Garrett wouldn't make it. Lindy reached into her pocket, pulled out the bracelet, and slipped it over her trembling hand.

Don't think about it; just do it. She took a couple of steps back, ran forward, and leaped off the edge.

"No!" Garrett yelled.

Lindy willed herself to float. She looked down and wished she hadn't. Vertigo hit her as the vast landscape spread out miles below. Her queasiness nearly made her start falling again. Concentrating on saving Ashton, she floated down.

"I can't hold on!" Ashton lost his grip, screaming as he plummeted.

Lindy went into a horrible free-fall. Her stomach tried to come up her throat. The wind rushed into her face, whipping her hair around and making her eyes water. Ashton was right below her, but she couldn't catch up to him.

"Come on, stupid bracelet!" She turned and held out her arms in front of her, so her whole body was in a straight line, and propelled herself down faster. She reached out and grabbed his arm, then flew in a gentle arc until they were going up again.

"I got you." She pulled Ashton up and threw her arms around his waist, holding him tightly. He put his arms around her neck, and together they drifted back up to the sky island.

They floated up over the edge of the island and back down again at a safe distance away from it. Lindy's feet hit the ground, and she mouthed a quick, silent prayer of thanks.

Her parents and several other adults from the village stood a short distance away, their eyes wide. Her parents rushed forward to hug her and Ashton.

"It's magic," one of the villagers said. Several others talked among themselves in hushed tones.

"What happened here?" Lindy's father demanded.

"They were playing too close to the edge," Garrett said, "and Ashton accidentally got pushed off."

"Because Rynden was tormenting the younger kids!" Lindy shouted. She glanced at Ashton, still in his mother's embrace, but he seemed to be too much in shock to say anything.

"Is this true?" Father started to walk toward Rynden and his friends, who were almost cowering.

"Wait, Aison." A villager stepped in front of Father. "Before we do anything rash, we should all go to the village square and give our testimony to the elders. Magic has been used; it must be dealt with."

"Yes, of course." Father sighed. "Let's go."

As they walked back to the village, Mother fumed quietly. "Children's lives were in danger, and all they can think about is their anti-magic rules."

"Don't worry, Lindy." Father took her hand. "We'll be with you, no matter what happens."

"But you should have told us the truth," Mother added, "instead of hiding that relic from us and breaking the village law."

"I'm sorry," Lindy whispered, tears forming in her eyes.

* * *

An hour later, nearly the entire village had assembled in the town square. The five elders sat in chairs on a dais in front of the village fountain, and two ceremonial guards stood on either side. All the witnesses gave their accounts, including Lindy and Miki, who explained how they had found the bracelet. The elders conversed with each other in private for a couple of minutes, and then the Head Elder spoke to the crowd.

She was an older woman with a gaunt face. She wore an embroidered dark blue robe.

"We have heard the testimony, and we have concluded that the law against magic has been violated," she said. "We must consider the penalty."

"Maybe we should consider whether this is an outdated law." Father stepped forward. The crowd murmured at his audacity. "I fail to see how my daughter's magic use is a threat. In fact, it saved my son's life."

"After his life was put in danger by an elder's son," Mother said, also addressing the elders.

"That matter will also be dealt with," the Head Elder said. "And your daughter's valour is noted, Aison and Kessie. Considering the circumstances, we have decided she will not be punished. However, the relic in question must be destroyed." More murmurings went through the crowd.

"But the bracelet belongs to my family." Lindy surprised herself by speaking up. The elders all looked straight at her, and she almost lost her composure. "Our family crest was on the box we found it in. And it could be really useful. Why do we have to be afraid of magic?"

The Head Elder raised an eyebrow. "Those are valid points. But it seems many in Skyvale misunderstand the reasoning behind our laws. Our founders did not outlaw magic out of fear and prejudice against forces they did not understand. On the contrary, they understood those forces all too well. They enacted this law because people are weak and sinful by nature, and no one is pure enough to be trusted with power of that kind."

Lindy didn't expect this development. *So they didn't fear magic, after all?*

The Head Elder continued, "In the old days, we had Guardians who protected the people by wielding powerful weapons of magic, but they eventually became corrupted by the power they held and by the desire for still more power and control over others. Our ancestors enslaved and killed many while using magic to govern others, even when it started with the noblest of intentions. That is why our founders relocated to this sky island. We are not so foolish as to believe we can eliminate the undesirable parts of human nature, but we can, and will, take steps to minimize their consequences.

"Now the accused will relinquish her talisman to the Council, and it shall be delivered to the smithy to be destroyed."

Lindy's throat was tight, and she was glad she didn't have to say anything else because she thought she might start crying. It wasn't so much that she was losing her bracelet as it was the humiliation of it all. She looked at her father, who nodded. For a brief moment, she had a crazed urge to fly away from the whole village. Nobody could stop her.

She brushed the thought aside and took a deep breath. Stepping forward, she slipped the bracelet off her wrist and handed it to one of the guards.

"This council is adjourned," the Head Elder said. Some people in the crowd dispersed, and others formed into knots and began talking.

Maybe the old crone has a point, Lindy thought. *A magical relic probably isn't going to turn me into a power-hungry maniac, but it might make me worse than I am. I've already broken the village law, let my parents down, and ignored my friends and family. And it might be even worse if a bully like Rynden owned it. Was my ancestor one of those tyrants, and did he hide the bracelet only to keep it safe so he could go back and reclaim it later?*

Miki approached her. "I'm sorry you lost your bracelet, Lindy. And I'm sorry I had to testify against you. I would have kept it a secret."

"I know," Lindy said. "I should be the one apologizing to you. It's probably better this way, anyway."

"But you saved your brother's life," Miki said.

"Yeah, but if I had kept my promise to him instead of fooling around with the bracelet, his life wouldn't have been in danger to begin with."

"I'm just glad you didn't get in bigger trouble."

"Thanks for not saying 'I told you so'," Lindy said.

Miki smiled. "Hey, let's go get some appleberry juice. You deserve it after that ordeal."

"Good idea," Lindy said. "But only if they don't put mushrooms in it like they did last time."

* * *

Later that day, Lindy was at home washing dishes when she heard the village bells ringing. Before she had time to wonder what was going on, Ashton came running in.

"Lindy, there's a pirate ship coming!" he shouted.

"A pirate ship?" Lindy felt a chill go through her body. "Are they attacking us?"

"I don't know."

"I'm going to go see what's going on." Lindy put down the dish she was drying.

"Father said to stay here," Ashton said. "He'll be here in a minute, and then we're all going to go hide."

"I'm going to the square." Lindy ran out the door, ignoring Ashton's protests.

As she got close to the village square, there was a great hubbub; bells were clanging, and people were running around and shouting. Miki and Garrett ran toward her.

"Lindy, we've got to go hide!" Miki said. "There's a pirate ship coming!" She pointed up toward an airship hovering over the woods between the village and the Dropoff. It was lined with wicked spikes around its hull, and a great horned skull jutted from its prow. Lindy shuddered at the sight. *They sure aren't trying to hide the fact that they're pirates,* she thought.

"Isn't there something we can do?" Lindy said. "Can't we fight them?"

"We don't have enough trained warriors in the village," Garrett said. "We'd be slaughtered."

"If only the elders hadn't destroyed the bracelet..." Miki trailed off.

"They didn't," a voice said behind Lindy.

She turned around and saw Rynden holding the bracelet in his outstretched hand. He looked down at the ground, not meeting Lindy's eyes.

"But... how?" Miki said.

"My father was going to take it to the smithy to destroy it," Rynden said. "But they weren't ready yet, so I sneaked in and stole it. They haven't figured out who took it. It belongs to your family, Lindy. You should have it." He held it out.

Lindy hesitated. *Do I really deserve this thing? And do I want to get in trouble again?*

"Also, I feel bad about what I did to Ashton," Rynden said. "I'm really sorry."

The apology made up Lindy's mind. She took the bracelet. "Thank you."

"Look, the pirates are coming down!" Miki pointed. "Let's go!"

The ship had a huge, round air bladder attached to the top deck, allowing it to float. Tiny figures climbed down ropes hanging from the ship.

"Why are the pirates getting off the ship so far away instead of flying right over the town?" Lindy asked.

"They probably don't want to get in range of our mounted crossbows," Garrett said. "If the ship was close enough, one of those big bolts might be strong enough to pop that air bladder."

Lindy had a sudden mental image of Ashton popping a gas plant with his slingshot, and the plant being propelled backwards.

"I know what to do," Lindy said. "Garrett, give me your dagger."

Garrett looked at her quizzically, but he pulled his dagger out of its sheath and handed it to her.

"What are you going to do?" Miki said.

Lindy gripped the bracelet and the dagger with resolve. "I'm going to save the village."

She slipped the bracelet on her wrist, shot up in the air, and curved toward the ship, holding the dagger out in front of her with both hands. The wind stung her eyes, and she could hardly see where she was going. The ship rushed toward her at a terrifying speed. She had to be quick, before the pirates had a chance to defend their ship. The bladder looked extremely tough and probably couldn't be penetrated by a simple stab. The bracelet would give her the extra strength she needed—she hoped.

Lindy braced herself as the dagger pierced through heavy canvas and leathery hide, while her body collided painfully with the side of the bladder. An arrow from below flew by and grazed her hair. With a yell, she quickly ripped sideways with the dagger, slicing a huge gash through layers of material. A blast of air came out of the bladder and pushed her away. Screaming, she tumbled backwards. The airship was propelled away in the opposite direction. Some of the pirates still clung to the wildly swaying ropes, while others plummeted to the ground.

For a moment, she almost lost consciousness, but she regained control of herself. Using the bracelet to slow down her fall, she landed in the middle of the village square, tumbling across the cobblestones. Miki ran toward her and helped her to her feet. Villagers streamed back into the square and gazed at her in wonder. She was dizzy, her legs felt wobbly, and she had numerous scratches and scrapes. Garrett approached her, his mouth wide open.

"I believe this is yours." Lindy held out the dagger in her outstretched palms.

Garrett took the dagger and held onto one of her hands. "Lindy, I… I've been wanting to say…" he stammered.

Don't think about it. Just do it. She moved forward, stood on her tiptoes and kissed him on the lips. Garrett's face reddened and a silly grin spread across his face.

"Actually, that's exactly what I've been wanting to say," he said. They looked into each other's eyes and laughed.

They were interrupted by other villagers congratulating Lindy for her bravery and thanking her. Her mother, father, and brother came and threw their arms around her.

* * *

A short time later, Lindy heard about the other details of the incident. According to a few witnesses, the pirate airship had been blown completely away from the island and had crash-landed somewhere in the forest below. Lindy wondered if any of them had died, and the thought made her uncomfortable. The few pirates who had already disembarked from the ship at Skyvale had been easily captured. They were banished, two or three at a time, to the Lands Below with the Head Elder's small personal airship. Some of the villagers had wanted them thrown off the Dropoff, but more merciful voices had prevailed.

The elders assembled in the town square, and Lindy once again stood in the place of the accused.

The Head Elder stood up and adjusted her robes. "Thanks be to the Creator that we were delivered from the pirate scourge. After the events of today, the council of elders has realized the need for strength and power to defend the innocent against those who would do us harm. There will always be the temptation to abuse that power, but that is a necessary risk. As long as pure and honourable people hold that power, perhaps the risk will be lessened. And so, we have decided to repeal our ban on magical relics, if the village is in agreement."

The crowd shouted their affirmation.

"Furthermore," the Head Elder continued, "we are hereby appointing our first Guardian in many generations; one who has already demonstrated inestimable courage and wit in defending Skyvale: Lindy Honeytree. What do you say, Lindy?"

"I don't know." Lindy felt the eyes of every villager on her. "I'm not sure if I really want all that responsibility."

"That is precisely why you should have it," the Head Elder said.

"Then I accept." Lindy meant to sound determined, but it came out as more of a frightened squeak.

The crowd exploded with applause. Many of them gathered around to congratulate her. Miki and Garrett walked up to her, both smiling.

"What have I gotten myself into?" Lindy said. "I'm scared."

"Well, you always said you wanted to do something big," Miki said.

"And you won't be alone." Garrett took her hand.

“You’re right.” Lindy already felt reassured, and she squeezed Garrett's hand.

“I just hope those pirates don’t come back.” Miki looked up at the sky.

“If they do, then we’ll be ready for them,” Lindy said.

Miki nodded. “So, what are you going to do, now that you’re a Guardian?”

“First, I think we should all go pick some mushrooms together.”

Alex has been reading since before he can remember and writing almost that long. He has published more than 20 books and is author and editor at his imprint Celticfrog Publishing. He lives in Kamloops with his dog and the stories clawing their way out of his head.

His most recent project is the new 'Blue in Kamloops' series, with the first book Tranquille Dark being released this spring. For more information and samples see alexmcgilvery.com.

Aggie's Sword

By Alex McGilvery

The chill of Dozmary Pool had penetrated far enough for Aggie to decide to get out. The unusual warmth of the English sun had sent Aggie paddling in the nearby pond. Her father was napping, the first rest he'd had in the months since the babies had come home. This picnic, away from squalling twin baby brothers and the constant urge to help, was to celebrate her move to Year 7 and a new school.

She splashed back to where she'd climbed into the pond, a microscopic bit of beach. Something stung her foot, and the surprise made her fall face first into the water. It tasted mossy, and not at all nice.

Sitting up, Aggie looked at her soaked shirt, now marked by blotches of green algae. She twisted her leg to inspect the bottom of her foot. A scratch more than a cut—not enough to wake her dad.

Aggie crawled back, feeling with her hands for whatever had toppled her. A long, narrow thing took shape beneath her fingers, with enough of an edge to make her wary. Another piece crossed the first, then the thing became cylindrical. She couldn't budge it from her kneeling position, so she stood one foot on either side of the round bit, got both hands around and heaved.

It wouldn't move, so she tried again, and it wiggled just a little. Once more then. The thing came up out of the water making a squelching noise. Her arms wouldn't stop lifting it until she held it high over her head, where it dripped stinking mud on her face and hair.

The sword—Aggie had watched enough movies to recognize it immediately—blocked the sun, and for the briefest second it looked as though it had flashed with brilliant light. Then the weight of the mucky sword made her arms tremble and she fell to her knees.

A croaking voice startled her. "Well it ain't a rock, but it'll do. Awfully foolish way to choose a leader if you ask me."

Aggie let the tip of the sword drop back into the water and looked around for the source of the voice. The only living thing besides her and her dad was a rather large toad, which jumped off into the grass as soon as she'd met its eyes. She shrugged and stood, wiping mud from her face, then limped toward the sand, holding her find with both hands, sticking it into the muck, stepping, moving the sword. Her foot hurt worse now.

At the shore, Aggie rinsed the mud from the sword and herself as best she could. Then she tossed the sword onto the grass and sat on the bank to push herself out of the water with her uninjured foot.

With most of the muck sloughed off the sword, Aggie could see it was plain, with no gems or anything else to relieve its utilitarian lines. She stood up and hopped toward her dad, using the sword to keep her balance. She puffed for breath, vowing again to exercise more and lose weight—or at least turn it into muscle.

"It's a sword, for Pete's sake, not a crutch." The same cranky voice came from the grass. The toad glared up at her.

"You going to carry me up the hill?" Aggie pointed at the toad with her free hand. *A talking toad? Maybe I've had too much sun.*

"That wouldn't be wise." The toad bobbed its head. "My apologies." It jumped along beside Aggie until she reached her still slumbering father. She dropped to the ground beside him and used a napkin from the basket to clean the cut, then wrapped another one around it, tying it on top of her foot.

"Am I really talking to a toad?" Aggie looked around for the toad but couldn't find it.

"If that's the strangest thing to happen, you'll be lucky." The voice came from further away this time.

"Who are you talking to?" Her dad woke up and stretched. He saw the sword in Aggie's hand and stared. "What on earth is that?"

"A sword. I stepped on it wading in the pond." She waved her hand at her bandaged foot.

"What do you plan on doing with it?"

"Well, I'm not throwing it back." Aggie ran her fingers along the flat of the blade. "Maybe someone at the museum will know more about it."

They packed up the remains of the picnic, with Aggie eating some of the food left over from earlier then tossing the rest into the tall grass.

"We'd just have to throw it out anyway," she said when her dad raised his eyebrow. He nodded, then picked up the basket with one hand and offered the other to Aggie. She lifted the sword in her left hand, then limped to the car with her dad's arm around her waist. He made her put the blade in the boot.

***

Their first stop was at a chemist's, to buy proper gauze and tape for her foot. With her shoes on, the cut hurt less, so she made her dad drive to the museum in Bodmin, where she carried the sword in to lay it on the desk where a woman stood arranging brochures.

"I'd like to talk to someone who can tell me more about this." Aggie tried not to giggle at the woman's wide eyes. Her name tag read Karina.

"May I?" At Aggie's nod, Karina picked up the sword and held it carefully while peering at the blade and hilt. "Doesn't look very old," she muttered. "Machined, not forged. The wrap on the hilt's too even."

In the woman's hands, under her inspection, the sword didn't look as real as it had dripping mud into the pond.

"I found it in Dozmary Pool."

"If this was Excalibur, you'd be the Queen of England." Karina grinned at Aggie. "I expect it's a movie prop. We've had our share of King Arthur movies here because of the legend." She put the sword down on the counter and handed Aggie a booklet. "You can keep it if you like, or leave it here."

"I'll keep it, thank you." Aggie put her hand on the sword.

"Careful," Karina said, pulling out a tag and writing on it. "Get too deep into the Legend of King Arthur and it will consume you. I've got three different history degrees, and I still want to learn more."

"Wow." Aggie picked the sword up, trying to emulate the way Karina had handled it. It felt right in her hand. "If I have questions later, can I call you?"

Karina wrote something on the back of the tag. "There's my email. Ask away. Maybe send me a picture of it when you've cleaned it up; I can hang that in the museum here. Keep the tag, it certifies I've looked at it and said it isn't something the Antiquities people need worry about." Karina walked with them back to the car. Aggie put the tag in her pocket and the sword in the boot.

"Thanks for your help." Aggie waved as she climbed into the car. As her dad put the car in gear, Aggie looked over at him. "Now we need to convince Mum to let me keep a four-foot sword in my room."

"Don't look at me. It's your sword." But from the look on her dad's face, he was already planning what to build to display the find.

***

Aggie had misjudged her dad. He'd bought her a book on King Arthur. A thick one with footnotes. The sword leaned against the corner of her room as she slogged through the book. Keeping her find entirely depended on reading through the tome. That was what Jenny had called it. Aggie looked at the book through the afternoon light with much more interest than the sword itself.

Jenny sat in the corner, her feet tucked up into what had to be the most uncomfortable position, reading her own book on Arthur. She flew where Aggie plodded. They were the perfect opposites, Jenny with her black belt in Taekwondo, Aggie with a belt that no longer made it around her waist. She could have gone on to compare hair, skin and everything else, but what was the point?

Jenny had welcomed Aggie the first day in Year 1 with a brilliant smile, as she had every year since. Six years later they were inseparable. Aggie only wished this extended to the others in the class. After Jenny's board-breaking demonstration no one bullied Aggie, but neither did they go out of their way to be friends.

"Aggie Farrier, you're moping again." Jenny's eraser bounced off Aggie's book. "The book isn't that hard. It isn't like you have to write a report."

"My dad keeps asking me what I've learned." Aggie stretched, holding the book tightly in her pudgy hands. Her toes had already been bruised when it slipped from her grip.

"Well, what have you learned?"

"Arthur was this kid who pulled a sword from a stone and became King, only no one can agree on what sword or what stone. The movies show him in armour, but the book says he lived way before armour like the knights wore was invented. He had a bunch of knights who went on quests and did all kinds of weird things."

"That's a start." Jenny grinned at her. "Think your mum would let us try cutting some water bottles out back?

"She's out cold with the twins, but Mrs. Hathway will throw a fit." The old woman was their neighbour on the council estate, who had no hesitation expressing her opinions on proper behaviour.

"It's Friday, she'll be at the pub a while yet."

"How do you know these things?" Aggie stood and put a bookmark in the book. It wasn't even close to the quarter mark. *Oh well, swinging the sword has to be more fun than reading.*

***

They filled bottles from the recycling bin with water and balanced them on a stump behind the house, the final remnant of what had been the last growing thing in the tiny backyard.

Jenny went first, as it was her idea. She swung the sword like a bat and launched the bottle into the gate to the alley.

"Oops. It looks easier on YouTube."

Aggie took the sword and tried to hold it like one of the diagrams in her book. Her fingers tightened and she stepped forward to slash at the bottle.

"You missed." Jenny giggled, then gasped as the top of the bottle slid away to land with a splash on the dirt. "I didn't think it was that sharp."

Aggie tested the edge with her thumb; still the not-quite-sharp it had been when she found it.

***

They spent the rest of the afternoon cutting bottles. Jenny got to the point of cutting them in two as they launched, but Aggie's strikes always looked razor-edged. She could slice a bottle into rings before it fell.

The slam of a door warned them Mrs. Hathway was home, so they cleaned up and returned to Aggie's room to study the sword more.

"You think it might actually be Excalibur?" Jenny ran her fingers along the blade.

"Right." Aggie snorted and stood it in the corner. "The museum lady said it was all the wrong shape and stuff."

"If it had looked real, what would have happened?"

"She would have kept it; there's some law or other. Dad looked it up."

"Agatha." The shout came from downstairs. "Can you help with the boys?"

"Sure, Mum." Aggie shrugged at Jenny. "I'll see you tomorrow."

"I have a tournament." Jenny packed away her books. "It's at the Rec, so you can come and watch if you want."

"I'll ask Mum."

***

After watching the twins all next morning, Aggie was allowed to head down to the Rec to cheer Jenny on.

People of all ages and shapes in white uniforms crowded the place. A couple of moms were talking about a rumour that the council housing had been sold. Aggie was tempted to stay and listen in, but she didn't want to miss Jenny's match. She found Jenny covered with red foam armour beside a mat. A girl on the far side wore blue. A wide smile lit up her ebony face as she trotted out onto the mat.

"Wish me luck," Jenny said. "She's *good*."

"You can take her." Aggie slapped the red armour.

Jenny flashed her a grin and went to meet her opponent.

They bowed to each other, then the round started. Aggie couldn't follow the flurry of kicks, but once in a while a scorer would hold up a red or blue card.

By the third round, they were tied and the crowd was cheering wildly. At the end of the round, the other girl landed a solid kick which sent Jenny staggering back onto her butt. The bell rang for the match. The other girl went over and helped Jenny up. Aggie ran out from her side.

"*C'est domage*, you fought well."

"I've never lost before." Jenny took a deep breath. "That was brilliant." She went into a discussion of the match, which lost Aggie within the first few words.

"I must go. My coach will wish to speak to me before my next match. My name is Lamkay."

"Jenny."

"Aggie."

The girls turned to look at her and she reddened.

"Lamkay, Aggie is my best friend." Jenny put a hand on Aggie's shoulder.

"I'm sorry you came out to see your friend lose."

"If Jenny isn't worried about it, I'm not going to. We'll look up your match and cheer you on." Aggie grinned at Lamkay.

"Right, you have to win now. I want to have been defeated by the champion." Jenny slapped Lamkay's back.

"I will do my best."

Aggie lost her voice before the end of the day. Lamkay won the championship and Jenny the B side tournament.

"Come back to my house for ice cream," Aggie begged them.

"Sure thing."

"Where do you live?" Lamkay's coach asked.

***

The four of them ended up in the coach's car to drive up to Aggie's house. She worried suddenly about her mum's reaction, but the twins were playing quietly and her mum was in a good mood. They took the ice cream out back.

"You're very good," Lamkay's coach said. "As I'd expect of someone from your school. Sensei Joe is a terrific instructor. I've been trying to convince Lamkay to join your school. She needs a different instructor to round her out, and since she moved here, it's much closer."

"So, should I join yours?" Jenny asked.

"You can, but better yet, just drop in to visit once in a while. Keep us on our toes."

"I will do as you ask, Sensei." Lamkay jumped up and nodded. "Now that I've seen how good Jenny is."

"Could I join too?" Aggie put a hand over her mouth, but glared at Jenny and Lamkay's giggles.

"Black belts should have more respect for learning." Sensei Mack's voice didn't get louder, but the giggling cut off and the girls blushed deep red.

"Taekwondo is expensive." Aggie's mum collected the dishes.

"She can come out for a few lessons before she has to pay," Jenny said. "I'll talk to Sensei Joe."

"We have some spare doboks; Lamkay will bring one by for her."

Next thing Aggie knew, they were teaching her the basic stance. It made her legs tremble, but Aggie bit her cheek and endured. The praise of her friends, old and new, was better than ice cream. She had to wonder why she hadn't asked before.

***

The end of the summer vacation arrived, and Aggie walked to school. A block from her school, she saw a crowd of boys around someone on the ground. She jogged over, marvelling that she could move faster than a walk after just a couple of months. When she recognized Lamkay, her fists clenched.

"Back off, Ben—and your cronies too," Aggie yelled. The biggest boy turned and laughed.

"If it isn't everyone's favourite tub of lard." He looked around for Jenny, then grinned.

"Really, Ben. That's the best you can do? Sad, sad, sad." Aggie had no idea where the words were coming from, but she wasn't about to stop them. "After all this time, you can't come up with something original?"

He stomped over to her, fists clenched. "I don't have to listen to your tripe."

Aggie put her hands on her hips. "Go ahead and hit me." She stuck her chin out, heart pounding as he towered over her. These words, she wasn't so happy about.

"Do not touch her." Lamkay walked around to stand beside Aggie.

"And what are you going to do abo—"

"She beat Jenny for the Championship at the Rec." Aggie grinned at him as he stepped back. His buddies snickered and Ben frowned.

"Why didn't she beat me up then?" He cracked his knuckles. "Maybe this Taekwoncrap isn't—"

While he was nattering, Lamkay jumped and kicked out, flipping the cap off his head. He paled and stumbled away, his gang following him.

"Thanks."

"*Merci.*"

They spoke at the same time, then laughed and sauntered after the boys.

Jenny met them at the school outside the gates.

"I saw Ben and his boys practically run into the school."

"Aggie took him down a notch." Lamkay opened and closed her hand, like it was talking.

Soon after they settled into class, the headmaster called Lamkay to the office. When she didn't immediately reappear, Aggie stood up.

"I should go to the headmaster; I'm a witness. It will save time." The teacher waved her on and returned to history.

***

Ben scowled as the secretary ushered Aggie through the door. Lamkay stood head down and hands clenched behind her back.

"—using martial arts is very serious." The headmaster frowned at Lamkay.

"Sir," Aggie winced ready for a rebuke for interrupting, but the words poured out of her. "I expect Ben didn't tell you how he was pushing her around before I got there and she didn't hit back, nor that he was thinking of hitting me when she stepped up to my defence. Probably not that he was ready to start a fight, when she kicked his hat, not his head."

With each word Ben turned redder. "Of course, the girls are going to stick together."

"You didn't mention Aggie's presence." The headmaster frowned and Ben's red face became white. "We spoke about this. You can't be bullying students. I'll let the coach know."

"Please don't kick me off the rugby team." Ben all but fell to his knees. His eyes actually glistened.

"Kicking him off the team won't help." Aggie said. "His problem is that he has too much time. Make him coach the juniors or something." She laughed at his gobsmacked expression. "He can eat lunch with me and learn how to make conversation."

This new mouth is going to get me killed.

"Very well." The headmaster pointed at Ben. "This is your last chance."

***

At lunch, Ben came over to their table. Jenny and Lamkay frowned at him, but Aggie slid over and patted the seat.

"Ben is turning over a new leaf." Aggie giggled at the dumbfounded looks from her friends.

"I thought you were joking." Lamkay shook her head. "So, what are we talking about?"

Ben had to be reminded more than once that insults didn't count as conversation, but when the subject turned to rugby, he brightened and became part of the dialogue, not just a sullen observer.

***

Over the next month Aggie spent lunches learning about rugby, Taekwondo, and Lamkay's home country of Cameroon. Ben's friends came by to tease but ended up joining them, though Aggie had to pull him back into his seat a few times. Life was as good as Aggie thought it could get.

Then the paper came out with the headline.

Local council housing to be demolished.

"Where are we going to live?" Aggie demanded at the dinner table, her stomach in a knot.

"We're looking for a place." Her dad sighed. "We might have to sell your sword to help get the deposit. We have three months."

Aggie went upstairs and fetched the sword. She put it on the table, anger and fear pulling the knot tighter.

"Here it is, if you need it."

"Thank you, dear, but it doesn't belong on the table." Her mum smiled and dabbed her eyes. "Put it back in your room for now."

Aggie stuck the sword back into its corner, somehow disgruntled that it hadn't immediately solved the problem.

"Don't be thinking you can give Excalibur away that easy." The voice from the pond came from under the bed. "That's what they want. Take Excalibur and take your power."

"Power?" Aggie flopped in her chair. "I haven't got any power." *I forgot about that talking toad. What's going on?*

"All those new friends... You don't think you did that on your own?" The voice's compassion took the sting out of the words. "Of course, you aren't used to such things in this day."

"I'm supposed to believe that chunk of steel is magic..." Aggie trailed off as the sword glowed briefly then changed shape. Now it was shorter but deadlier looking, more like what the illustrations in the book showed. Then blinked back to the familiar blade and she rubbed her eyes.

"There are more things than you can imagine with power to change the world."

"What am I supposed to do with it? I'm not killing anyone."

Laughter came from beneath her bed. "You won't be killing; far from it."

Whatever was under the bed left. Aggie could feel its absence, but it would be back. Maybe it was Merlin. Merlin always knew what King Arthur needed to do.

***

Aggie wasn't very good at Taekwondo—the warm-up was torture, she could hardly kick above her knees, and sparring was terrifying. Her reward came at the end of the class, when they broke boards. She loved smashing the wood into pieces. Her hands stung briefly, but it never stayed; and when she stomped on the boards, the shock of the break never made it past the heel of her foot.

She wanted to try the bricks, but the often-bloodied hands of the black belts held her back.

"You are improving rapidly." Lamkay rolled up her belt and put it in her bag, then folded the dobok before putting it in too. She never wore it outside the dojang. Jenny and Aggie walked to and from the dojang in their doboks.

"Why don't you wear the dobok home? You wouldn't sweat as much without the extra layers."

"I was born in Cameroon. Sweating is a reality of life." Lamkay laughed. "In Douala, there were boys who would challenge anyone they saw wearing a dobok. It is hard to avoid fights, so I never wore it outside. *C'est la vie*."

"What was it like moving from there to here?" Aggie blushed; maybe she shouldn't be asking.

"Douala is a big city, so a lot of things were the same. But a lot of things were different too. There, I was the normal looking one, and some days I wished to look different. Here, I stand out..."

"But you're beautiful," Aggie said.

"So my father tells me." Lamkay grinned. "It is not so hard now I have good friends." She hugged Aggie and kissed her on the cheek.

***

They walked home, talking about the class. Aggie could follow the conversation now, but she mostly listened. A notice in a shop window caught her eye.

"Look, a Mr. Mori from the company who's redeveloping the council homes is coming for a public meeting."

"That's going to be trouble." Jenny frowned, clenching and unclenching her hands. "A lot of people are angry."

"Mum and Dad aren't; they're looking for a new place. I told them they could sell my sword for the deposit. We may even get a bigger place."

"Sell your sword?" Jenny's frown deepened. "I guess, if that's what you want."

"What I want is to help my family." Aggie's stomach boiled. "It's not like it does anything but collect dust in my room."

"Helping your family would be stopping the redevelopment." Jenny rounded on Aggie. "My mother has a petition she's taking to Council."

"Good luck with that," Aggie rolled her eyes. "It had to be their idea in the first place."

"What do you know?" Jenny shouted at Aggie and ran off.

Aggie moved to follow, but Lamkay put a hand on her shoulder.

"Friends fight; I argued with my friends when we were moving to England. I wish we had made up before I left."

"It's my fault." Aggie's eyes leaked hot tears. "I should have known Jenny and her mum would fight it; they can't afford to move."

"Perhaps we need to aid their fight." Lamkay took Aggie's hand. "Come, we'll talk to my father." She dragged Aggie away from the window. Lamkay's hand was hot in Aggie's, and Aggie reddened as she saw people from her school. *No, I've already hurt one friend today.* Aggie relaxed her shoulders and walked with Lamkay. Once she stopped worrying about it, holding hands was pleasant—not like she imagined it would be with a boy, but easy, a connection between them.

***

Lamkay stopped in front of a law firm and Aggie's eyes widened.

"It's okay, my father doesn't mind visitors." They found out from a woman at the counter that he had a couple of minutes between clients, if they didn't mind waiting.

"Please do not speak of anyone you see in the office." Lamkay put a finger on her lips. "Confidentiality is important."

"I won't." Aggie peered around the waiting area, too open to be called a room. Expensive-looking paintings hung on the wall, and the chairs were leather and steel. The men and women wore clothes Aggie thought her parents might wear out on a special night.

"Did you and your friends hold hands in Douala?"

Lamkay dropped her hands and looked down.

"*Je suis desolé*, I forgot it is different here."

"I'm not upset, once I stopped worrying about it, it was... nice." Aggie lifted her chin. "And if it reminds you of your home and your friends, I don't mind."

"Mr. Batoum will see you." A woman came out from behind the counter to speak to them.

They walked into his office—not as plush as the waiting room, but Aggie liked it. Vivid paintings hung on the wall, along with sculptures she was sure he'd brought from Africa.

"Hello, you must be Aggie." He smiled, brilliant and warm like Lamkay.

"That's right." Aggie grinned back. "We wanted to ask you about the development."

Mr. Batoum's smile faded.

"I'm sorry, but I can't talk about it."

Aggie opened her mouth to ask why, but Lamkay put her hand on Aggie's knee.

"We understand, Pappa." Lamkay stood. "I am glad you got to meet Aggie."

"So am I."

They left; this time Lamkay didn't hold Aggie's hand as they walked down toward Aggie's home. Lamkay's shoulders shook, then she sniffled.

"What's wrong?" Aggie stopped and took Lamkay's hand.

"The only reason Pappa wouldn't talk about something is if they were a client of the firm." She threw her arms around Aggie and sobbed. "*Mon père est un ennemi.*"

"Listen, you can't help who your dad works for. We can still help Jenny."

Lamkay shook her head. "It would embarrass Pappa."

"He should be embarrassed." Jenny stood red-faced across from them where they'd turn toward Aggie's home. "He's helping them." She threw a ball of paper at Lamkay. "And you," she poked Aggie in the chest with a hard finger. "Traipsing about holding hands like a daft kid. I don't want to talk to either of you again."

She stomped off, curses floating back to turn Aggie's ears pink.

Aggie picked up the paper then stood, trapped between the fire in her veins and the ache in her heart.

"It is hard, *mon amie.*" Lamkay's voice broke. "It was so, when I moved. The rage, it burned in my friends. They felt I'd abandoned them."

Aggie smoothed the paper. It was a petition with no signatures on it. "I'm not leaving it this way," Aggie vowed, her heart burning. "We've been friends since forever. I'm not letting something as foolish as this be the end."

"You are brave, Aggie." Lamkay hugged her, then walked away.

***

Aggie went home, filled up all the plastic bottles, then fetched her sword.

Slicing the bottles into thin rings wasn't as satisfying as when she'd done it with Jenny. *Why did we only do this once?* When she ran out of bottles, she started attacking the stump, slicing it down until a tiny green leaf standing out from the stump made her pull her cut.

Just like the fight between her and Jenny. A little bit of carelessness, and look what happened. She threw the sword into the corner of the yard with a clatter.

"It isn't the sword's fault." Mrs. Hathway's voice made Aggie's blood chill. She turned to her neighbour. *I'm in for it now.*

"Please don't tell my mum."

"What, that you are slicing bottles and stumps into slivers, or that you tossed the blade away like trash?"

"You're right, it isn't the sword's fault." Aggie went to pick up the sword and examine it for damage.

"It would take more than that to dent old Excalibur," the toad voice said.

Aggie spun, almost dropping the sword. An immense toad sat on Mrs. Hathaway's shoulder. "It was you under my bed?" It puffed up and looked ready to explode.

"Relax, Albertus, she didn't mean to insult you."

"No, no." Aggie tucked the sword under her arm and came over to the fence. "You are a fine figure of a toad. I've just never had the privilege of conversing with one such as you, at least not knowingly."

"Well, ye got the gift of the gab alright." The toad deflated.

“Come have tea. Bring the sword.” Mrs. Hathway opened the gate.

Since when was there a gate there?

Her neighbour’s lips twitched.

“Let me clean up my mess.” Aggie put the plastic in the bin and tossed the sliced-up bits of wood into the corner of the yard with the weeds. “There, that’s better.”

“Indeed, it is.”

***

Mrs. Hathaway’s home shouldn’t have been much different than Aggie’s, being the other half of the semi. But it felt larger and cozier. A small fire burned in the grate. Mrs. Hathway used a cloth to lift a kettle from the fire and pour water into a teapot.

“You’ve been doing marvellously so far, dear, but the hard bit is about to start. Don’t turn back.”

“What am I supposed to do?”

“I can’t tell you that.” Mrs. Hathway poured tea and handed a cup to Aggie.

“Use what you’ve learned,” Albertus grumped from the cushion he sat on as though it were a throne.

“Now, would you like milk or sugar?” Mrs. Hathway asked in a tone which made it clear the subject was closed.

“Neither, thanks.” Aggie picked up the cup and inhaled the perfume of the tea. She sipped at it.

“How do ye know it ain’t poison?” Albertus asked.

Aggie deliberately took another sip while she considered her answer.

“I don’t, I guess, but what would be the point?” She shrugged.

“To take Excalibur from ye, dimwit.”

Aggie picked up the blade and offered the hilt to Albertus. "Do you want it? All you need to do is ask."

Mrs. Hathway laughed as the toad scrambled back.

"I keep telling you it isn't about the sword, but the person."

"What kind of queen offers to give away 'er sword."

"Aggie's kind."

"Wait, queen?" Aggie put her cup down. "Queen of what? We already have a queen."

"Of course, dear—you did draw the sword after all."

"From mud, not stone, and the lady at the museum..." She picked up her cup and took a long sip. Her heart slowed and she could think more clearly.

"It is the drawing. You will learn in time of the rest."

"Right." Aggie examined the sword closely. "In my room, when Albertus was talking to me, it looked different for a moment."

"It takes what appearance it needs to."

"What would happen if I did give it away?"

"It depends on why." Mrs. Hathway stared into her cup thoughtfully. "If it thought you were dishonouring it, it would vanish, and you'd have a much harder time being queen. If the reason were honourable, it would find a way to come back to you."

"Okay, that makes sense."

Aggie finished her tea, lost in thought.

***

She didn't see either of her friends at school the next day or the next. The first lunch alone with Ben felt awkward, but he didn't treat her any differently.

On the third day, he asked why Jenny and Lamkay weren't around.

“It’s complicated,” Aggie said. “We had a fight, and I don’t think any of us know how to start to make up, so we just kind of keep drifting further apart.”

“You can’t let an argument break up the team.” Ben looked at her seriously. “Everyone gets angry or stupid at times, just look at me.”

“I don’t think you’re stupid, Ben. You just needed a nudge to see things a new…” Aggie trailed off. “You’re brilliant.” She jumped up and kissed him on the cheek before dashing away, then saw a poster on the bulletin board telling the community that Mr. Mori would be talking to the people from the council housing at seven o’clock that night.

Aggie drifted through the afternoon alternating between chills of excitement and a hollow dread. By the time they were dismissed, she felt sick.

“You don’t look so good.” Ben came up. “Maybe I should walk you home.”

“But you’ll miss practice.”

“I’ll explain to Coach. You wait here.” Five minutes later, he was back, and they started down toward her home. Their fingers brushed together and Aggie took hold of his hand. His strength settled her, so by the time she got home, she could smile at her mum’s shocked face.

“Thanks, Ben.” She gave him another kiss on the cheek. “It means more than you know.” Ben walked off—was he *skipping?*

“I’m going to the meeting tonight,” Aggie said. “Can we have supper early?”

“Sure, I think.” Her mum shook herself. “We’ll have a talk when you get home, right?”

“Of course.” Aggie headed up to her room, where she picked up Excalibur. “Could you try to look like something which won't get me arrested?" Excalibur shifted into a butter knife. "Great!"

***

There was a large crowd in front of the council building. Aggie went around to the back. A single light illuminated the door and the path to the parking lot.

"What are you doing here?" Jenny stepped out of the shadows to hiss at Aggie.

"I figured you'd be here." Aggie took the butter knife out of her pocket. "I came to help."

"What?"

"You're here to confront Mr. Mori, maybe bruise him a bit if he won't listen."

"What of it?" Jenny's chin lifted.

"So, I'm going to help." The butter knife became the sword. "This will do the job properly."

"Are you crazy?" Jenny tried to push the sword out of sight. "You'll get arrested."

"And you wouldn't?" Aggie gave a twisted grin. "You know what I can do with this thing."

"But you're all right. You don't have to worry about losing your home. I have no choice. We can't find a new place; we can barely afford the dump we have."

"My sword is at your command." Aggie held it up. "Tell me what you want."

"I want you to go away," Jenny said. "You can't do this."

"You're my friend. If we go to jail, we go together."

Jenny stared at Aggie, then fell to her knees. "I'm so scared, Aggie. I don't want to be homeless."

"What is going on?" A tenor voice spoke from behind Aggie.

"Friend stuff." Aggie held the sword out. "Can you hold this for a moment?"

"Uh, sure." A tall man in a suit looked at her uncertainly before taking the sword and peering at it.

Aggie knelt beside Jenny and wrapped her arms around her friend.

"I know it's scary. For years, you stood between me and what I was afraid of. Now it's my turn. You won't be homeless; you can have my room wherever we go."

"I'm an idiot."

"Everyone is sometimes."

"Very true." The tenor voice said. "Did you know this is the sword from the 1998 *Arthur and the Vampires* movie?"

"It is?" Aggie looked up. "That's nice. You can have it if you promise me something. Whatever happens, my friend and her mum have a place to live."

"I see. Perhaps for your friend's sake, I should rethink the way we are planning the development." The man was still examining the sword. "Mr. Batoum did suggest we could stagger the work so there is less hardship on the people. We do plan to build some units for the Council's use. It won't add much to the cost, but it is priceless in P.R just as being seen to make families homeless would be a disaster. I will have a word with him before we start. Maybe we can fast track their new home "

"Mr. Mori," came another voice from the shadows, a deep bass matching the huge man who sauntered up to them. "You are running late already."

"Right. Halad, could you put this in the trunk for me?"

The big man took the sword, making it look hardly bigger than the butter knife Aggie had been carrying.

Mr. Mori knocked, and the door opened to let him in.

“You know I wouldn’t have let you harm Mr. Mori,” Halad rumbled at Aggie.

“I sort of expected you’d be here, or someone like you.” Aggie stood and helped Jenny up. “But she’s my friend, you know?”

“You have quite a friend there,” Halad said to Jenny. He looked at Aggie. “I’m going to put this in the trunk. When I get back, you won’t be here, right?”

“No, sir.” Aggie took Jenny’s hand and dragged her away to the front. Lamkay stood forlornly outside the door. She brightened as Jenny and Aggie ran up.

“I was worried I’d missed you.”

“Your dad is amazing.” Jenny flung her arms around Lamkay and spun her in a circle.

“He is?”

“He suggested a way for Mr. Mori to change things so we won’t have to live in the car.”

“We had a little chat with the man,” Aggie said.

“A chat—you offered to chop him into pieces!”

“He didn’t seem worried,” Aggie said. “He was more interested in the sword than anything else.”

“And Aggie gave him the sword in exchange for him making sure we aren’t ever homeless. I was an idiot. Do you forgive me?”

“But of course.” Lamkay grinned broadly. “Without you and Aggie, I wouldn’t have had the courage to call my friends in Douala and talk to them.”

***

Ben grinned as he sat down.

“Good to have you back, ladies.” He gave Aggie a quick hug before digging into his lunch. Her friends stared at her open-mouthed. Aggie winked at them.

"Oh, I saw this in a shop, and for some reason I had to buy it for you." Jenny held out a tiny, bejewelled sword brooch. Aggie pinned it inside her jacket.

She reached across the table to her friends.

"I have something to show you at home."

After watching Ben practice, the four of them walked to Aggie's home, where she led them past her mum to the yard.

"Look." She pointed at the stump. "I diced up all the bottles, then I sort of got mad and chopped up the stump, but now…"

The remnant of the dead stump was covered in green shoots.

Blazej Szpakowicz was born in Warsaw (Poland), grew up in Ottawa (Canada), and earned a PhD in history from Cambridge (England). Over the years, he's spent an awful lot of time in London—albeit a slightly less post-apocalyptic version than he presents within these pages. Nowadays, he's back in Canada, where he works as a professional editor (at http://www.bplusediting.com) and amateur language nerd. He reads voraciously across a wide range of genres, writes weirdly, and wishes he had more time to do both. This is his first publication; he's had some variation of the story in his head for years and is glad that one of them finally got out.

The Knife in the Stone

By Blazej Szpakowicz

She should've known it was a con.

After all, *Whosoevereth pulleth this swordeth out of this stoneth*...? Nix was no expert in old English, but it seemed a bit... over-*eth*ed.

And Mr. Sagan had been so confident. "Nicolette," he'd said, "This is it. The big one. Best job in a bloomin' decade." And he meant it. Nix had known him for more than half her fifteen years; she could tell when he wasn't lying.

"Archaeological relics," he'd said, "from the old days, before the Fall of New Camelot and the Fae Invasion."

"A king's hoard," he'd said, "Literally. Lost Arthurian treasures."

"The sword in the stone," he'd said, eyes glittering like coins.

Except the stone was a lump of plastic and the sword was a knife with a bog roll taped to it. A nice knife, long and sharp with a white bone hilt—but no Excalibur.

Mr. Sagan would not be happy, which usually ended badly for someone. Nor would Jinny, Nix's sister. She'd been characteristically enthusiastic when she learned of the job. New Camelot had become a bit of an obsession, ever since Nix had "acquired" her that old library book, with all the pictures.

And it'd seemed so promising. The Lock-Vault was harder to get into than the queen's knickers: heavily fortified, well-guarded, with state-of-the-art security tech. The sort of protection usually reserved for proper valuable stuff.

But the Great Hero's armour was as plastic as his rock, his shield was painted wood, his treasury was old rail tokens. Apart from the knife, the sensors in her ocular overlay confirmed, everything was 100% genuine ersatz.

Well, 'twas better than nought. At least she could take the knife. It'd come in useful—she'd been working unarmed for months now, ever since the police at Kingscross had "confiscated" her viral dagger. (And she'd never even used it!)

Right, time to go. She toggled her infrareds, then peeked into the dark passageways outside the vault. No visible movement. Faint footsteps a few corridors away, but no one immediately around. As safe as possible, under the circumstances.

She squeezed past the door and carefully slid it shut. To her horror, it locked with a loud, ominous thud. She froze, barely daring to breathe. The distant footsteps paused momentarily, then, too quickly, started once more—in her direction.

Lovely! They'd be on top of her within minutes. Not enough time to re-open the door, or to get out of the long, straight, uncluttered corridor.

She crossed to a shallow alcove behind a bulky corrugated pipe—not much of a hiding spot, but the best available. The footsteps approached ever nearer, accompanied by a jaunty, off-key whistle (was that some old-timey tune her Mum used to sing her, back when she had a Mum?). With a shiver, she pulled her climate-controlled leather jacket close and wished she'd made her hair a slightly less electric shade of blue. Her hand slowly wandered down to the knife.

After a moment, the whistling paused in mid-note, and a peaked cap and shiny row of buttons bobbed into view. The man inside them was old but fit, with a severely broken nose and a superannuated mechanical leg. His left eye blinked neon red as he scanned the corridor before him.

He stood maybe a foot away from her. Nix silently mouthed a prayer, tightened her grip on the knife, mentally begged the old man not to see her...

...and he didn't. He just blithely walked right past her hidey-hole, oculars sweeping back and forth without pause.

She almost laughed.

***

Nix took the long route back to Mr. Sagan. Bad news was always best delayed. Her lateness was at least plausible: the Lock-Vault was in Waterloo, after all, right in the heart of Londongov territory. And the route back to Camden passed through the City (Jonny Crosstown's turf; he hated Mr. Sagan) and Islington (the Enoch brothers'; they hated Mr. Sagan too).

Over the course of the journey, Nix almost convinced herself she'd just imagined the near-miss with the old security man. She'd simply been lucky, yeah? Maybe the bloke was careless, maybe his oculars were busted, maybe he just didn't want to fill out paperwork.

But then it happened again. Twice.

First, there was the stereotypical Rozzer—blue-coated, be-truncheoned, monolithic—loitering at Piccadilly station just as Nix needed to change trains.

For obvious logical reasons, Nix preferred to avoid the police. They didn't usually kill nowadays (part of Londongov's big clean-up act), but they had no compunctions about less fatal forms of violence. And they tended to treat people who looked like Nix as criminals even when they weren't actively committing crimes.

She'd ducked back just before he glimpsed her. There wasn't time to get away (again!), so she simply did what she'd done in the Lock-Vault: backed up against the nearest wall, pulled the knife from her belt (just in case) and fervently hoped the Rozzer wouldn't see her.

And (again!) he didn't. Not as he stomped toward her, not when he paused at a burnt-out shop stall right beside her hiding spot, not when he stopped at the end of the platform to survey a pavement well-pounded. He stared unseeing directly at her, then nodded in satisfaction and went on his way.

Something weird was going on.

An hour or so later, she ran across Kris, her ex. One of her more tolerable exes, admittedly—harmless, easy on the eye, all-round decent, just unable to deal with Nix discovering who she really was. There'd been a lot of that, depressingly, and the wound still festered. There were probably people she had even less desire to run into, but Nix couldn't honestly think of any.

Time for an empirical experiment. Was something really going on with her new knife, or had she just been insanely lucky twice in one day? She gripped the hilt tight, concentrated and quickly strode past Kris...

...who never even blinked. It was like she was in-bloody-visible.

She finally arrived at the Firm as evening fell. She couldn't see the sky through the enviroshields, of course, but the lights were just switching to dark mode.

The encroaching night made the complex look even more eldritch horrory than usual. It'd already been the largest building in Camden when Nix first signed her indenture. The eight years since had seen it expand wildly, new corridors and annexes sprouting up as Mr. Sagan bought up territory and operations and people.

It always put her in mind of a parasitic weed.

***

Mr. Sagan, even gaunter and more predatory than usual, tsked as he surveyed the bounty across his mahogany desk. His Jarvis stood behind him, bald pate gleaming, arms clasped at its back. There was something haughty about its sunken eyes, despite the company boilerplate about techno-homunculus uniformity. A few standard-issue thugs, mostly redcaps and fear deargs, loomed in the corners of the room, doubtless to remind Nix who was in charge.

"Nicolette, m'dear girl," Mr. Sagan said, "I ain't no great expert on 'istory, but most sources agree Excalibur… is a sword."

"I know," Nix said.

"Not a knife."

"I know! But this was the best I could do—only thing in that vault of yers as wasn't a fake. I reckoned you'd want t'know."

"I'm grateful, of course, m'dear! Just a touch… disappointed. All the money and resources what went into this job…" Mr. Sagan tsked again and shook his vulturey head.

"It's all there was," Nix repeated firmly. "You can look at me phone recordings if you like. You know I always work kosher. I think yer contact spivved us."

Mr. Sagan spread his palms. "Oh, don't worry, m'dear. I know you've always done right by the Firm. Someone does seem to 'ave been less than entirely truthful with me…" His bone-dry voice trailed off, and Nix shivered. "But I don't reckon it's you. In the meantime"—He ran a long, white finger down the blade— "Well, I s'pose it could fetch a few bob, recoup some small part of me investment…"

"Actually, can I 'ave it?" Nix asked quickly. She coughed uncertainly as Mr. Sagan raised an eyebrow at her impertinence—after all, she couldn't very well say it was probably magical and she didn't want to give it up. "I mean… y'know the Rozzers nicked me last one, yeah? Been 'alf-naked ever since. Me sister's been worried I'll get meself killed if I keep on. I can—" She sighed deeply. "I can pay for it, if you like. Or you can take it out of me contract. Can't be more'n a couple days' extra work."

Mr. Sagan hummed thoughtfully. "I'll admit it don't look *too* valuable..."

Nix nodded diffidently. "Well, of course not. It's just a normal knife, not even wired or virally enhanced. And I ain't no use t'you dead or behind bars, am I, sir?"

For a moment, Mr. Sagan gazed at her through narrowed eyes, a cruel god surveying a struggling ant. Then he burst into a plastic smile that didn't even try to reach the eyes. "But of course, m'dear! After all, ain't I always been yer friend?"

***

Camden Market was an unholy hotchpotch of desiccated hovels, repurposed shop stalls, skeletonized vehicles and converted cargo containers—but home nonetheless. Nix and Jinny's flat (they always called it that, in a vague pretence of normality) was almost palatial: big and comfy with good insulation and electricals and space enough for two whole rooms.

The sisters sat in the bigger of the two, their bedroom-cum-living room. The white knife lay on a small table (read: packing crate) between them.

"Yer 'avin' me on," Jinny snorted. She had fluorescent pink hair today, and eyes some designer shade of indigo. Her cybertats, apparently indispensable for the computer stuff dominating her waking life nowadays, glowed faintly under her skin. "I mean, yer actual Excalibur, that'd be one thing, but..."

"I'm serious!" Nix said. "Watch."

Jinny snorted sceptically. But as Nix grabbed the knife and focused her mind, the younger girl's eyes twitched with sudden pain. "Ah! What did you..." She paused, blinked, wiped away tears. After a while, her eyebrows shot up and her head whipped around in a mild panic. "Nicky? Where are you?"

Almost at once, Nix released her grip. “Sorry, I didn’t mean to—”

“That was brilliant!” Jinny cut in, beaming widely. “You was like a big, black, shadow… blur… thing. Me eyes was just slidin’ off you!”

Nix released a held breath. “Believe me now?”

“I reckon I might just, yeah. So… what is it, exactly? Did New Camelot have any famous knives…?”

“I… don’t actually know,” Nix admitted. “I don’t recall no knives in the stories, and there ain’t no good public list of the relics.” She giggled as a stray thought crossed her mind. “Ooh, I know, let’s call up Londongov and ask t’look at their confidential records. Pretty please, lads, it’s all in a good cause!”

Jinny nodded. “Yeah, all right.” Before Nix could stop her, she tapped her temple to activate her ’phone and rapidly started to weave delicate patterns in the air. Her cybertats buzzed and glowed as she did so. Computer stuff.

Nix clapped a hand over her eyes. “Please don’t tell me yer doing what I think yer doing…”

“I would, but me big sister always tells me not t’lie. Anyway, why not? Londongov’s got the best records of Arthurian relics. It’s the easiest way t’find out what you’ve got.”

“I was joking, you daft twit! What if they catches you? They’ll—”

“Got it! Take a look,” Jinny cut in, tapping her temple again. Under her breath, she added, “Catch me? Please…”

A browser window opened in Nix’s optic overlay. She sighed. “Fine… Carn-wen-nan. Translation, little white hilt. The dagger of King Arthur, as listed in the Welsh traditions. Blah-blah-blah. Not in traditional English records, but existence officially determined in… Blimey, but they go on! Confirmed magickal powers: can… shroud its user in shadow. Oh. Wow. I take it back, yer brilliant."

"Yes, I am," Jinny said with a satisfied nod. "D'you know what this means?"

"Do I?" Nix echoed. "I can go anywhere, steal anything, spy on anyone. Could rule the bloody city, so I could!"

Jinny stuck out her tongue. "Actually, I were thinking you could finally clear yer debt with Mr. Sagan. Pull a couple real big jobs, give 'im with a whole boatload of sterling… Finally go freelance, like we talked about. All sortsa work out there for an invisible girl, yeah?"

Leave Mr. Sagan's Firm! Jinny made it sound so easy. But then, she had no debts, no indenture, no life experience—just a head full of stories. She'd never had to deal with the real world, like Nix did after Mum was killed. That skewed a person's perspective.

The thing was, Mr. Sagan did not encourage departures from the Firm. He treasured loyalty, in a one-directional sort of way; everyone knew he disliked traitors. No one had quite worked out his definition of treachery, but Nix had known people to vanish, have accidents or be conveniently arrested for petty reasons like starting unapproved side hustles or nicking merchandise. So she suspected that definition was rather loose.

***

She had to determine how Carnwennan worked, what its limits were. Test it out in safety, in public areas like the Regent's Forest settlement, the open rail lines, or the Kentishton walkways.

She quickly confirmed it worked against digital eyes as well as organic ones—after all, that very first security bloke had ocular implants, as did just about every Rozzer in London. Not surprisingly, it worked best at night or in the dark: people remained completely unaware of her presence unless she made too much noise or outright bumped into them. During the day, she had to concentrate harder to keep the shadows intact and people seemed more liable to sense her, but they still couldn't actually *see* her when she stayed focused.

After a few days, she stepped things up. Small scale stuff at first, nicking the odd bangle or viddisc or jacket. Nothing serious, nothing expensive. Her thievery still took work—Carnwennan didn't prevent alarms from sounding, nor did Nix want to leave securicam footage of stolen goods vanishing mysteriously into the æther—but it was definitely easier.

She also started poking around among Mr. Sagan's pigeons—Jimmy the Rat, who would sell anything to anyone, steal it back, then sell it again; Gerry K, with the shifty little eyes that noticed nearly everything; Stiletto Ling, who'd trained Nix in self-defence and now ran the Firm's protection rackets. She didn't actually *trust* any of them, but she needed contacts in order to make it on her own.

Next step: infiltration. Nix had always wanted to get into the Police Fortress at Kingscross, if only to know what they had on her. Now she could do so, in a less permanent way than usual for her sort of person. It proved harder than she'd hoped, as it turned out the Rozzers had bleeding-edge security and annoyingly observant personnel, but she'd pulled it off in the end—if just barely. It was not too useful, alas, as the Rozzers also had the inexcusable habit of pass-locking their computers, but still an interesting experience.

A couple weeks later, she returned with a thin, silvery disc Jinny swore could hack the Ministry of Defence itself. It turned out what they had on her was absolutely nothing. Mr. Sagan was on several watchlists, as were some of his more senior people, but she didn't even rate mention as a minor annoyance. Oddly disappointing.

Nix also learned Carnwennan could cover two, if they maintained physical contact. That gave Jinny a good excuse to cajole her way into much free ice-cream, a couple semi-legal tech-dens and a concert from her latest all-time-favourite band, the Illegal Somethings (their actual name, not a lapse of memory).

Twenty-two days after Nix found the dagger, they celebrated Jinny's thirteenth birthday by going to the most exclusive restaurant in Camden. Nix half-expected the boss waiter bloke to throw them out, but once he saw they had a reservation (created three days earlier by sneaking in under the shadows and hacking the computer), he grudgingly allowed them their reconstituted Pheasant à la Normande.

And finally, Nix went to see Mr. Sagan. She came unsummoned—likely enough in itself to set alarm bells ringing, as Mr. Sagan disliked having his time wasted. He would likely suspect something was up.

Care was called for. Tact. Delicacy. Mr. Sagan could not know she wanted out until Nix was absolutely certain she'd survive the revelation.

***

"So, you want to leave our little family, hmm?" Mr. Sagan asked, an avuncular smile on his lips.

Someone had told him. Probably Gerry K; never trust a man with shifty little eyes.

Nix crinkled up her face in confusion, then mobilized her most carefree smile. "Izzat what you've 'eard? I'm just planning for the future, is all! Exploring me options. I can't just go on working for other people for the rest of me life, can I?"

“Ah, well, of course not.” Mr. Sagan waved a hand airily. “And if you’d just come t’me and explained everything all proper-like, I’d be glad to ’elp! Until then, I’m afraid you do have a contract to uphold...”

“I weren’t planning not to!” Nix protested. “But that contract were for ten years, and I been ’ere now for eight. It’ll be up soon enough. I need t’start thinking past it, yeah?”

Another smile, sharp and thin as a razor. “Oh? Ten years of labour, that’s the terms of contract, yeah. But after raising you, training you, looking after that sister of yers, all those loans... Well, it might not be financially viable for me t’let you go quite yet...”

Nix’s eyes narrowed. “But... then ’ow long will it be?”

Mr. Sagan spread his palms wide. “Oh, who can say? It’s all so complicated... Meanwhile, seeing as you wants t’explore yer options, p’raps we could put you t’work elsewhere in the Firm? See what other little jobs you can do for us?”

Nix could imagine what sorts of little jobs he had in mind. Extortion, protection, wetwork... Those were the next steps up from her current role. Things to tie her to the Firm so closely she would only able to leave in a box. “No,” she said quickly, with unwonted honesty. “Sorry, sir, but as soon as me contract’s done, ’owever long that takes, I’m out. Y’know I’m grateful t’you, but... I need t’be me own person.”

Mr. Sagan’s smile faded for a moment, before returning twice as strong and half as convincing. “But of course, m’dear girl! The fledgling flies the coop! I wouldn’t dream of standing in yer way...”

***

Nix wanted to believe him, really she did. But a few things niggled.

For one, he'd been too honest, too straightforward. And Mr. Sagan was never honest or straightforward, except as part of a labyrinthine plot built on a house of lies.

For another, he wasn't as good a liar as he thought, especially to someone he'd all but raised. Nix knew when he was being honest (-ish), and this wasn't it.

For a third, she suddenly got lumped with a series of gentle, team-based jobs she could've sleepwalked through. "Training exercises," he said, lying through shiny white teeth.

For a fourth, she came home from the third sleepwalk to find her home and sister under attack.

***

It was more night than morning, maybe three o'clock. There were two of them. Man and woman, one thin, one fat, both ugly. The woman, tall as well as wide (maybe part cewri or buggane?), carried a DIY taser pistol. The man looked human, if oddly lumpy, and was, thank Goddess, unarmed.

Jinny sprawled against the wall, livid with bruises, one arm held at an awkward angle. Her cybertats blinked drunkenly.

They'd broken the door in.

The man, nearer the flat's outer shell, turned at Nix's approach, but she kept her composure enough to back away into the darkness and summon Carnwennan's shadows.

"What izzit?" the fat troll-woman called from within.

"I heard something," the man said in an echoey, Toff-accented voice. "Who is there?" His eyes wandered across the car park, but he gave no sign of having seen her.

Inside the flat, Jinny broke into a giggle.

"What're you so 'appy about?" the woman snarled, raising a sausagey hand in warning.

Nix flinched away from the ensuing slap, but it still echoed in her ears. Her knuckles tightened on Carnwennan's grip.

With speed belying her bulk, the woman now grabbed Jinny by the throat. "Oooh, I know, izzat yer freak sister out there? You think she's gonna save you?" The girl clawed helplessly at her assailant, who responded with a croaking rattle of a laugh. "Oy, Hom! See anything?"

The man stepped out into the car park and slowly, deliberately swept his gaze around it. His face barely moved. "No," he said at last. "Nothing." For a moment, he stood framed in the doorway, hands at his side, head raised inquisitively.

Stiletto Ling always told her to try to end fights before they could start. Try to hit a soft spot, an eye or ear or nose. Or neck. Nix took a deep breath, trying to focus her whole mind on maintaining Carnwennan's shadows, then leapt forward and swung the blade at the man's exposed Adam's apple. It was a near-perfect attack, slicing perfectly through with nary a catch. Ling would've approved.

But the man all but ignored it. Instead of doing the proper thing and collapsing into a heap, he just straightened back up, holding his near-decapitated head in place with one hand. "Perhaps there is something." Not so human after all. Hom, was it? As in *Hom*unculus? Jarvises weren't built for combat, but other models of techno-homunculus were.

Back in Nix's flat, the fat woman turned. "Whazzat, you big slabby git?"

Hom ignored her and took a ponderous step forward—right toward Nix, almost as if he could now see her. (Had her concentration faltered?) Before he could do anything else, she sprung forward and thrust Carnwennan at what remained of his neck.

The homunculus's body froze in place as his head (plus a few fingers) flew into the air, bearing an almost comical expression of surprise. "Well, really," he said.

The woman grunted and fumbled for her gun, but Nix had already moved in, slashing with Carnwennan. The woman just barely twisted away from the attack, which carved a gash into her torso. She grunted in pain, and her pistol clattered to the pavement. She staggered back a few steps then stopped, all a-wobble, eyes flickering between her gun and Nix's blade.

Nix followed her gaze uncertainly. Should she go for the gun herself? Probably smart, but it'd leave her open. Attack while the woman was distracted? Definitely smart, but she'd be outmatched in a hand-to-hand fight.

As Nix hesitated, the woman burst into motion. Nix barely avoided a beefy fist and tried to will herself back into the shadows—but the woman only winced in momentary disorientation, shook her head and barrelled forward. Nix tried to dodge again, but instead found herself slamming to the ground. A heavy blow crashed into her face, and something splintered.

She blinked dumbly, shook her throbbing head, and feebly tried to push the woman away, but couldn't properly raise her hands. She attempted to sit up, only to be overcome by a wave of nausea. Above her, the woman reared back for another strike.

There was a muffled fizz-bang. The woman froze momentarily, then twitched and collapsed, energy arcing over her. Hoist by her own zap gun.

Behind her, Jinny sat shivering against a wall, eyes wide and terrified, the woman's gun wobbling in her hands. "Oh God," she said like a broken record, "OhGodOhGodOhGod..."

***

"I'm sorry," Nix whispered. She'd lost track of how many times she'd apologized. They'd been huddled together now for... what? Twenty minutes? An hour? More?

She'd almost—

They'd tried to—

"They was working fer yer Mr. Sagan," Jinny said dully.

"I know nothing," Hom's head proclaimed from the tarmac. Nix had lost track of how many times he'd said that, too. Big slabby git, indeed. At least the troll-woman remained unconscious, thank Goddess.

Jinny's shoulders stiffened again. "They was waiting for me, Nicky," she whispered. "They said Mr. Sagan was... un'appy with yer plans to leave, that he wanted to show you the dangers of life outside the Firm..."

"This is my fault," Nix said with a sigh.

"Goddess, would you look at this place?" Jinny muttered into Nix's shoulder. "Nearly two years of our lives, and someone just... comes along and wrecks it."

"I'll call a cleaner..." Nix's voice trailed off, and she broke into a bitter laugh. "No, everyone I know works for 'im. We'll 'ave to get out of town. Bloody 'ell."

"How?" Jinny asked bluntly. "Don't yer smuggler friends work for 'im too?"

Right. Of course they did. Her whole bleeding world did.

"We could... ring the police?" Jinny suggested. At Nix's grimace, she added, "Look, what else is there? It's either them or the other gangs."

Nix snorted. "If I called in Jonny or the Enochs, I'd just end up working for them instead. And the Rozzers? Those pillocks couldn't find their backsides with satnav. Maybe if we dropped the whole blooming Firm gift-wrapped into their laps, but otherwise... I mean, these two ain't gonna tell 'em nothing."

"I have never heard of any Mr. Sagan," Hom chimed in, rather proving the point.

"No," Nix continued. "I think I'll have to... deal with 'im."

Jinny's eyes widened. "Nicky, you can't!"

"What, then?" Nix asked. "What else is there?"

"We'll think of something! I just..." Jinny paused, big, rabbity eyes tearing up. "You're me big sister. I don't want you t'be that sort of person."

***

Mr. Sagan had the best security in Camden. Passwords, deadlock seals, infrared cameras, motion sensors, enough armed thugs to overthrow a small country. But it had one minor design flaw: he didn't know people could be invisible.

The guards never noticed Nix stroll past them. Neither did the cameras. The sensors did register her movements, but knowing something's triggered a motion drone doesn't automatically allow you to see that something.

Nix slipped into Mr. Sagan's office just as he left for breakfast, which gave her an hour to root through his personal computer. With predictable hubris, he hadn't even bothered to pass-lock it—maybe he thought being hundreds of floors up behind unbreakable glass, an army of obedient servants and dozens of layers of security was protection enough. She quickly deleted all references to herself, then spent the remainder of the time skimming his files. They were painstakingly thorough, recording every job, every hit, every bribe, every bit of blackmail.

She'd just started reading about a hit on some bigwig toff up in Harrow when she heard voices. Hurriedly, she switched off the monitor and retreated to the darkened computer banks on the far side of the room.

"Is Mr. Charles back yet?" There was Mr. Sagan, in all his dusty-voiced glory.

"He is running late, sir." And the Jarvis, voice modulated to a tee. "A slight hitch has developed. He expects to unknot it forthwith."

Nix felt bad for the hitch—Rupe Charles was a Negotiator (blackmailer) and occasional Waste Disposal Specialist (hitman). His unknottings rarely ended well for the hitches.

The door buzzed open. Nix placed a hand on Carnwennan.

"And what of our... other little problem?" Mr. Sagan asked as he walked in.

"Still nothing, sir," the Jarvis said.

Mr. Sagan tsked. "Worrying. Rhudda is usually dependable, and the Homunculus bloke came 'ighly recommended." Ah, so the other little problem was her. Good to know.

"Perhaps we underestimated the girl, sir?"

Mr. Sagan grunted noncommittally. "P'raps we did. Right, follow up but don't let word get out quite yet. Too many people actually *like* her. Keep me informed."

"Of course, sir. Anything else?"

Mr. Sagan tapped his chin thoughtfully. "Yes... you can go 'elp the lads overseeing the Oxford branch. Some of the... employees is getting restless again. They need dealing with."

The Jarvis inclined its head then shuffled out. Once the office door had slid shut, Nix quickly toggled its deadlock seal. Best not to be disturbed.

When she turned back, Mr. Sagan sat reclined in his chair, staring off into the distance. "What're you up to, you little tranny bint?"

Nix's teeth ground together at the slur. She'd heard it before, of course she had. People were people. But she'd always thought Mr. Sagan was...

No. She couldn't get angry. She was here for a reason, time to act on it. She clamped down on her runaway thoughts, slowed her breathing, counted down to five—and revealed herself. "I told you what I'm up to. I want out."

Mr. Sagan sputtered, nearly falling out of his chair. "What? How?" For a moment, he just stared at her, jaw wobbling. Then, with a bare semblance of composure, he managed a weedy smile. "Nicolette, m'dear girl. I've been looking for you!"

"I 'eard," Nix growled, idly twirling Carnwennan. "Little tranny bint, was it?"

"Words spoken in anger, m'dear girl, pay 'em no 'eed!" Mr. Sagan smiled, fingers tapping nervously at his desk. "I were just a touch... distraught. I mean, trying t'skip out on our contract—after all I've done fer you!"

With a snort, Nix raised Carnwennan and calmly stroked its edge. Mr. Sagan gulped. The tapping of his fingers sped up, and his eyes flickered expectantly to the door.

"I hacked the deadlock seal," Nix said. "For privacy. Or locked it, anyway. Jinny did the actual hacking. I may have let her into the system a bit. You know, I was going to do this proper-like. Work off me debt. Figured it'd take months, years even, but I was gonna do it. Until you sent yer thugs after us."

"M'dear girl, I dunno what yer—"

"They were in me 'ome!" Nix yelled. "They hurt me sister! She could've—"

Her shoulders stiffened, her knuckles whitened, her lips curled into a grimace. Before Mr. Sagan could react, Carnwennan lay at his throat. Just one small thrust, just a tiny bit of pressure. So quick, so easy, so cathartic. She might even be able to get out safely afterwards, invisible girl that she was.

You're me big sister. I don't want you t'be that sort of person.

Carnwennan wavered. *No, neither do I.* Oddly deflated, she took a step back.

Mr. Sagan chuckled. "Aye, I thought so. You was always squeamish, girl."

"You don't want t'know 'ow close I just came," Nix said coldly. "You know, it's funny. I did come 'ere t'kill you. Jinny talks me down, convinces me there's another way… but with just three bloody words, you almost convince me right back again…"

"Please." Mr. Sagan's voice fair dripped with condescension. "I've known you half yer bleeding life, girl. Yer no killer. Yer too weak."

Nix shrugged. "Maybe. But it ain't me you've got t'worry about."

Mr. Sagan's eyes narrowed uncertainly. "What?"

Nix tapped her temple. "You get everything, Jin?"

"Oh, yeah," Jinny's voice chirped in Nix's ear. She must have patched Mr. Sagan into the conversation too, as his eyes widened slightly at the sound. "Easily. You've got *real* crap security, Mr. Sagan, sir. A hamster with a blunt penknife could hack yer systems."

"Who is that?" Mr. Sagan cried.

"That's me sister," Nix said. "Keep up. And this"—She stepped back to the computer banks and deftly removed a thin, silvery dot—"is a thingamaguffin she used t'get me into the Rozzers' database—"

"They's got much better security than you, bee-tee-dub," Jinny added.

"—and which also now has a copy of everything on yer mainframe," Nix concluded. "As does Londongov, all the free media, Jonny Crosstown, the Enochs, all yer other enemies, every underling polishing a knife fer yer back, and every private 'phone as just 'appened t'be online in the past five minutes."

Mr. Sagan swallowed nervously.

"Now, it's all real well hidden," Nix said. "Jin says it'd take years t'unravel, even if you knows what yer looking for."

"Years fer me," Jinny corrected. "More for normal people."

"Grease enough palms, maybe you'll be able to stop it from getting' out," Nix continued. "But go after me or me sister, and you'll be the most famous man in London."

"You bluff," Mr. Sagan said, voice cracking just a bit. "You couldn't possibly—"

—and then his computer monitor hummed to life, festooned with a cavalcade of photos, documents, emails, video and audio. The alert system on Nix's 'phone beeped in warning of a lengthy stream of new file uploads, a few of which popped up as previews in the corner of her overlay. (Nothing explicit, thank Goddess.) The way Mr. Sagan cast panicked glances at the empty air around him suggested it wasn't just *her* 'phone acting up.

"Every computer in yer office is seeing that," Jinny said sweetly. "Plus maybe a few just on the other side of the walls; it ain't an exact science, yeah?"

Nix backed away toward the door. "We're leavin' now. Dunno t'where. Somewhere sunny, probably. Jin always wanted t'see the sun. You've already paid fer our expenses—right generous of you, sir, we're undying grateful."

"You little brat!" With a sudden burst of speed, Mr. Sagan clicked a spot on his desk and pulled out a small black pistol—very old-fashioned, probably used actual bullets. Nix froze momentarily as he pulled himself to his feet and pointed it at her, shaking in fury. "You won't get away with this... this 'umiliation!"

Nix laughed, tightened her grip on Carnwennan, and focused her thoughts.

Mr. Sagan's eyes bulged and watered. "What...? Where did you...?" He wiped away the tears and fired off a blind salvo. The bullets embedded themselves into the door and walls, right where Nix no longer was. He whirled desperately. "Where are you? 'ow did you..."

"Wouldn't you like t'know?" Nix whispered into Mr. Sagan's ear. He twitched as Carnwennan poked into his back, and his own weapon clattered to the floor.

"What... are you?"

"Oh, no one special at all, sir," Nix said. "It's just there was something valuable in that vault after all, something real powerful. Sir. Sorry I didn't say. Anything 'appens t'Jinny, and I'll be back to introduce you."

Then she stepped away, saluted Mr. Sagan with Carnwennan and was gone.

***

Nix gazed up at the sky, shielding her eyes with her hand. The new sunglasses didn't help as much as advertised.

"I still ain't quite used t'that thing," Jinny said from beside her. "I think I always sorta thought it were a, wotsit, urban legend." Already adapted to the climate, she wore shorts and a cut-off top—and attracting more stares than Nix was comfortable with. (When had she stopped being a little kid? Could it be reversed?)

Nix was her usual leather-jacketed self, just with the temp-control turned all the way down. "I don't trust it," she muttered, squinting up again. "Or those melanoma vax. And that doctor bloke looked right shifty..."

Jinny poked her in the ribs. "Don't moan! It's lovely. And warm. I like warm. I didn't know I did, but I do. You did good, big sister." She grabbed Nix's hand, and Nix squeezed hers back.

And off they walked, under the burning sun.

Eileen lives in Kamloops, BC. She became interested in writing poetry and short stories while taking creative writing courses at the University of Waterloo in the 1990's. She has had poetry and short stories published in various anthologies and collections. Recently she has published an illustrated children's adventure/ fantasy book. She writes and performs in skits for local community groups.

The Endless Scroll

By Eileen Bell

Sarah felt like a nobody. Her mother ignored her. When her mother did talk to her, she often told Sarah she was no good for anything because she always walked around with her head in the clouds. When her mother said this, Sarah would look up, expecting to see her head somehow adrift from her body, her blond curls floating between the clouds, her face like a hollow oval between them. Sarah's mum would twist her lip, as in, *I told you so,* and walk away.

Her mom, Isabelle, was a teacher of languages at the local college. She was brilliant with languages, but as preoccupied with her career as Sarah's dad. Every once in a while, when Isabelle was excited or annoyed, she would drop a word from another language into her speech. Sometimes when Isabelle was behind in her class work, Sarah would help her organize and correct the student's assignments. So Sarah gradually picked up some words from other languages and made a list of the ones she found interesting.

One night her dad came home with an Irish wolfhound pup whose legs were too long for his body. Her dad left the pup on the kitchen floor, said a few words and left the room. After a day or two, no one else bothered with him. This bashful animal grew quickly into a bristly haired dog. He became Sarah's best friend. *We are two of a kind. Casualties. I am always being told to be more sensible. The dog isn't sensible. Is the house sensible? Certainly my family isn't sensible.*

Sarah lived in a two-storey, rounded house (sort of round-more like a rabbit warren, with narrow walkways between each new round, (or sometimes square-like additions) near the woods with her parents and her younger brother, Aaron. Her dad, Henry, was an architect who had built the basic house during a period of enthusiasm several years before. The later additions came in sporadic spurts. The house hadn't changed now for a few years. Drafty windows, floors that dipped and shifted with the weather, doors hanging from loose hinges. Sarah's mom was always complaining about the state of the unfinished house, or the much-needed repairs.

She would stand in the middle of the kitchen floor, hands on hips, calling in her shrill voice, "Henry, Henry, the floors shifted again. How do we eat at a lopsided table?"

If he answered, he would say, "It's not the table Isabelle, it's the floor."

She shouted back. "Of course, I know *that,* Henry."

Henry would smile and nod and slip quietly into his work room, making plans for other people's houses, muttering over his drafting table, ignoring anyone who opened the door to his room, hoping for a short conversation.

"Must get this drawing finished. Now where did those blueprints get to?"

When he wasn't working, he was rushing out of the house with a hasty wave, papers fluttering from his briefcase.

Sarah would watch him sadly from the porch, as he reversed his rusted car onto the twisting road into town to present his ideas at some important meeting. He nearly always smacked the family mailbox as he was backing out. He would strike it, shrug, smile at Sarah and continue squealing and lurching his car as he drove away. The mailbox stood like a monument to their mixed-up house and family. Dented and misshapen, but surviving.

Her eight-year-old brother was annoying her this morning—the first day of summer break, Sarah's last summer break before High School in the fall. *Tagging after me when I just wanted to be alone. Annoying questions... Always with the annoying questions and the big words.*

"Let's go check out that pine tree again, there's something mysterious and otherworldly about it, Holy thieving, cackling monkeys, maybe there's a secret entrance, or maybe a dragon lives inside, just waiting to be set free. Holy thieving cackling monkeys."

"You're just a silly boy. What is so strange about a large tree? What eight-year old boy uses the word, 'otherwordly' and in the next sentence says maybe a dragon lives in the tree?"

"I do, and I know what otherwordly means better than you do."

"Get lost, quit following me around. Find your own friends."

"I don't have any, neither do you."

"Will you get lost! I'm going for a walk with the dog. You can't follow me. Mom said you're not allowed in the woods by yourself."

"I won't be, I'll be with you."

"No you won't."

Sarah walked slowly along the path leading into the woods. Aaron wouldn't come after her, at least not right away. *Aaron is right, I have no real friends. I wish things were different. I wish I had a happier family. Maybe then it would be easier to make friends. I don't know.*

Her dog, now full-sized, loped along beside her. "Come back, Infinito," she called when he ran too far ahead of her down the trail. *My favourite word these days.* She sighed. *The Latin word for love. At least my dog hears the word love spoken out loud.*

A few yards ahead in a clearing, Sarah could see Infinito frantically scrape his paws over the mushy surface of the ground near a tall, old pine tree with wide, flowing branches.

As she approached the circular clearing, a feeling came over her. She had experienced this before when she and Aaron had visited this spot. *It's like stepping into another world. Aaron is right. Why am I so mean to him sometimes? It is no excuse, but I don't want to share this place or anything about it with anyone, especially not with my brother.*

"I wonder what mother would say about this?" she asked. "She would likely say something funny and sarcastic about me having the company of a tall tree when my head was stuck in the clouds." The dog howled up from the tree base, UhoooOOHhOO, looked over at Sarah and then began digging at the ground under the tree.

Then Sarah forgot all about her mother, the dog and the clouds.

"Salve, Sarah ac Infinito." A deep, gravelly voice came from somewhere above.

Sarah, taken by surprise, tripped backward over a broken branch beneath her feet. She lay sprawled on the ground looking up. She thought she saw a vague shadow of a man hovering behind the branches. *Am I hearing a voice, a Latin voice*? *No, must be my shaky imagination. I wish Aaron was here to hear this.*

"I heard it too, Sarah. Aren't you glad I'm here?"

Aaron stood behind her, grinning mischievously. His face was smudged with dirt and his stringy, red-blonde hair hung in his eyes.

"You followed me! Oh, never mind that. You heard the voice coming from the tree?"

Before Aaron could reply the voice came again.

"Ego beatus sum in occursum tibi Sarah et Aaron et Infinito." The tree bent its lower branches toward the dog, who was still scratching at the earth.

"Et invenies in fi nito volumen solitudines sempiternas."

This time Sarah was sure the voice came from the tree itself.

Sarah stood up and brushed off her clothes, feeling braver now. "Did you say something, Mr. Tree?" She tried again to see the shadow.

The shadow looks like it's floating behind the pine needles. Trees don't have tongues or mouths, so how can they talk?

"Narrito est nomen meum."

"Can you speak English, Mr. Tree? My brother doesn't know Latin and neither do I. Actually, I do know a few words."

With this, Narrito gracefully bowed his branches toward the children. Then he folded his pine needles toward his trunk, pointed his treetop downward and drew into himself. When he was finished, he resembled a long, narrow green pole with prickly bits sticking out here and there. The children stared up in amazement. The shadow had disappeared completely.

"I think the tree just introduced himself to us, Aaron."

"Holy fire-breathing dragons."

"Where do you get those weird expressions?"

"How do I know? I'm eight years old."

He shrugged at his sister and then looked over at Infinito. "He's found something."

Infinito was excited now, barking and trying to pull what looked like an old, torn, dirt-encrusted book out of a hole in the ground. Sarah picked up the book.

"Just a tattered old book." She flipped a few pages. "Looks like Latin words, and Wow- Look at these beautiful, old-fashioned illustrations." Then she looked up at her brother. "Do you think Mr. Tree, Narrito, is telling us to read this book?"

"I don't know why he would, and why Infinito would dig it up? Does he know more than us?" At this, Infinito began prancing around with his head up.

"He seems pleased with himself." Sarah knelt and hugged her dog around his neck. He whined happily into her ear. "I love you, Infinito, let's go home."

Sarah strode toward home down the narrow path, ahead of her brother and the dog, holding tightly onto the book. Aaron skipped along behind her. Infinito trailed further behind, sniffing the ground.

"Who's going to keep the book? Hey, maybe it's a book about dragons?" Aaron asked as he dragged a stick along the path.

"No dragons-I'm keeping the book. Quit dragging that stick in the dirt and hurry up. Mom will be wondering where you are."

"Ah, she don't care when I come home. She's always got her nose stuck in some funny book, and Dad's always off somewhere working. What are we going to tell Mom and Dad if they ask what's going on?"

"Nothing at all," Sarah answered in a snooty tone. "We need to be sensible about this."

Sarah needed time to think—to be sensible, as she had told Aaron. She didn't see any of these events as sensible, but she had to put him off, until she figured out what to do.

At home she went quickly to her room and locked the door. She lay across her bed letting out a long deep sigh. *What is this? What is this?* She sat up, staring at the book. Every time she tried to open it, an eerie shiver crawled down her spine. The cover was heavy as lead, and she was unable to open it.

That's odd. I could easily open the book in the magic circle. The magic circle... That's it! The clearing is a magic circle around the tree! I can't let Aaron see the book until I know it's safe. What if I read it and it turns out to be full of something evil? I didn't get any feeling that the tree was nasty or malevolent, to use one of Aaron's big words. What did the tree really say to us? I'll have to borrow Mom's English-Latin dictionary to figure that out. How can I do that when I can't remember all of his strange Latin words? Maybe I could just figure out what he wants from his gestures. He did bow his branches as he was talking and Infinito was digging up the book. I think he wants us to read the book. But how can I read it if the book won't let me open it? Maybe I'll see if Aaron has any ideas.

Isabelle appeared at the bedroom door, wearing an apron. "Dinner is on the table. Hurry, dear, we are waiting. Then she asked in a sweet, but somewhat irritated tone. "What's that book on your bed?"

"Oh, nothing much, just a bit of summer reading." Sarah put the book onto her shelf, shoving it under some other books.

"Come along then, dinner will be cold."

Are we eating together? Eating as a family? she asked herself after her mother closed the door. She paced up and down her room, twisting her long hair around her pinky finger. *What is going on? She called me dear. Is she feeling well? I'll talk to Aaron after dinner about what to do with the book. What am I thinking?*

***

Henry had gone to another meeting, and Isabelle was dishing spaghetti from a pot on the stove.

Aaron was clinking his spoon and fork together at the table and singing,

"Dad lives in his briefcase.

Pokes his head out now and then.

He eats spaghetti with a pen."

Isabelle scowled at him as she handed him a plate of spaghetti. "Stop crowing that nonsense and eat your dinner."

Sarah slumped, a few strands of spaghetti hanging from her fork. Her other hand was against her cheek and she leaned her elbow on the table. She was as disappointed as her brother that her father was not at the dinner table.

"So, how did you two lazy kids amuse yourselves today?"

"Oh, we just went for a quiet walk in the woods." As Sarah said this, she glared at Aaron across the table. While their mum was looking down at her plate, he shoved a big forkful of spaghetti into his mouth then grinned sheepishly at Sarah, running his index finger across his mouth and bulging cheeks to show he understood.

Sarah thought this would be a good time to ask her mother if she could borrow her English-Latin dictionary.

Her mom thought for a minute. "I guess so. Are you kids up to something?" Without waiting for an answer, she continued, looking half-accusingly at her daughter. "Better your head in a book than in the clouds."

Later, with Aaron sitting beside her on the edge of the bed, Sarah tried to open the book again. The cover wouldn't budge.

"Aaron, try opening the book. It won't open for me."

He grabbed the book from her lap. "Gimmeeasy, easy."

The cover refused to open.

"Maybe we can ask Mom or Dad."

Sarah looked Aaron in the eye and shook her head sadly.

"Go to bed. We'll talk tomorrow."

Sarah woke suddenly in the middle of the night, as a strong wind and rain slashed and banged against her open window. She quickly pulled the shutters closed. A tree crashed in the distance.

"Narrito. I am worried about Narrito. I need to go to the magic circle and see if he is okay. What if he is cold and wet and damaged?"

She slipped on a pair of rubber boots. Infinito took the book from the shelf and dropped it at Sarah's feet. He whined anxiously.

"No! I can't take the book. I can't risk getting it dirty or lost. You can come, as long as you don't go running off into the night." She got up, put the book back on the shelf, then opened the window shutters and climbed out into the cold night. The dog stuck half out the window, hanging over the sill. She tugged him by his collar, then they were off into the night, leaving the shutters banging in the wind.

Sarah wore her raincoat and a sweater over her pajamas, but this was not much protection against the weather. The wind whipped and grabbed at her, whirling her about, but she persisted and found the path through the woods.

This is my adventure, mine and Infinito's. Maybe that's where I went wrong. Aaron, and especially our parents, don't need to be in this with me. Imagine Aaron even saying we need to ask mom and dad about the book.! No, I'll figure this all out myself. But first I need to see if Narrito is still standing as tall and straight as his Latin name.

She hurried along. A soggy raven squawked miserably from high in a tree. A mouse, or a vole, ran between Sarah's feet. She looked down, then tripped and fell on her behind in the wet debris on the path. The light from the full moon had broken through the sky's misty veil.

Sarah smudged her muddy, wet hands over her face and then tried to rub the dirt off her face with her sweater sleeve. A large raven poked her beak through a pile of wet leaves and branches.

"I lost my babies in the storm. They fell out when a wind gust blew it out of the tree. I think this is the remains of my nest. You too are like a lost child fallen from the nest too early. If you're worried about Narrito, he's good. Tall and strong enough to survive the storm. Remember how he wrapped himself up like a skinny pole. I'll make sure you get home okay. Your mom will be worried."

Sarah should have been surprised by this nosy bird who talked like a person and knew so much, but suddenly she felt tired. She had enough strength though, to insist on going on. "I'm going to see Narrito. I could be in my warm bed, but instead I am sitting on a forest path in the middle of the night arguing with a rain-soaked raven."

A rumbling chortle came from the raven's throat. Sarah shivered and water dripped from her hair and clothes. *Maybe that's her way of laughing.*

"We could look for my babies along the way to your home."

"Find your own babies- I'm going to the magic circle." She started down the path.

"You forgot to bring your book." The raven called after her. Infinito's long legs carried him leaping down the path. The raven tried again. "How about if we go back to your house and spend the night, then come back to the circle in the morning with the book?"

"You know about the book?" she said as she turned to where the raven was standing. Her shoulders sagged under the weight of her concern for Narrito and her determination to press on. Her resistance was nearly spent, but Sarah didn't wait for an answer from the raven. She began to run down the path.

She tripped, got up and continued stumbling down the dark, twisted path. Infinito was right behind.

When she neared the clearing, the raven was nowhere to be seen. She came to a sudden halt as a huge, wild-eyed, hawkish bird, wings outstretched, blocked her path. It had gnarled, pointy toes, like a chicken but much larger.

"Go home," it screeched, wings flapping, eyes menacing, screeching, talons close enough to scratch Sarah's face. A strange thought came to her as she faced this bird. *Maybe this is Aaron's imaginary dragon come to life. A bird or a dragon or both? Not going to talk about this to him anytime soon.*

Infinito stood frozen for less than a minute, then turned and took off, ears flying behind, legs moving so fast they were a blur. The moon shone perfectly round and cold overhead. She followed behind her dog, screaming. "Infinito wait for me."

***

Meanwhile, back at home, Isabelle had heard the noise in Sarah's room and had gone to investigate. She found the shutters flapping and closed them. Then she noticed the empty bed.

"That good-for-nothing girl has flown the coop and taken that flea hound with her."

Isabelle saw the Latin book lying on the shelf. It fell open before her. She was still reading the book when she heard Sarah returning. Turning, she stood beside the window, hidden in the shadow created by the bedroom light above. Infinito and Sarah talked outside the window.

"I wonder if the raven found her family, Infinito. Where did that horrible creature come from? All of a sudden it dropped in front of us like a scene from another world." Sarah was shivering and shaking. "I wonder- no, not possible." Infinito whined and looked up at Sarah. I think Aaron is right again. I think in a strange way you know more than we do."

"Oh look, the window is shut. Mom must be in my room. We're in big trouble!"

Beside the window, Isabelle's mind whirled. *Sarah and the mutt. Are they nuts? That book was written for me. It's all about me. Strangest stuff I've ever heard. Asking me questions I don't know how, or why, I should answer. Who wrote the stupid thing anyway? The book is written to me. Damnedest thing. Why would the kids have hold of it? Good thing it's in Latin. Sarah can't read it. What a laugh when I tell her. I'll have to trick her into telling me where she got it. Whatever nonsense she's up to. The kids are good-for-nothings just like their father.*

Sarah knocked on the window. Infinito began barking frantically.

"Go 'round the front." Isabelle called. "Door's open."

Aaron ran quickly around to the front door and came stumbling into the harsh light of the bedroom, rubbing his eyes.

"Where's Sarah?" asked Isabelle sharply.

Right behind Aaron came Sarah and Infinito. Sarah stood inside the door looking around the room, feeling hesitant and uncertain. Infinito headed straight for the safety of the cramped space under Sarah's bed and peered out anxiously. Sarah saw the book open on the bed.

"You took the book," she cried, staring in horror at her mother. "That's my book. How dare you?"

Then she realised her mother had been reading it. She grabbed the book off the bed and began to read it out loud. The text was in Latin, but Sarah was able to understand it perfectly.

"What is your life purpose at this time? What is a home if it is only rooms and doors and windows? Why does Henry stay away from home so much? Your children are a sacred trust from God. Treat them as such."

There was more text, but it was obscured. Sarah knew then what the book's purpose was. She knew the reason it had come into their lives. The book's text began changing. There was a brilliant light coming from the pages, which obscured the text as the words disappeared and reformed. She wanted to drop the book but held on tight. The book, the title of which she could see now was "*The Language of Love*." There were beautiful engraved illustrations throughout the book. There were pictures of mothers, fathers and children in beautiful pastoral, seaside and home settings, always looking on and helping one another with kindness and love.

The text had finished its transformation. Still in Latin. She read out loud.

"Who is Sarah? Where does she belong in the world? Who are her real friends? Find your true path. Discover your own Magic Circle. Don't be afraid. Love your family always."

Simple words, yet for Sarah they were surrounded with a shimmering light. She felt the light encircling her own being. She felt powerful for the first time, and with this power came glimpses of true understanding.

"Give me that book. It's mine. You stupid girl, where did you get this? Answer me!" Isabelle screamed in Sarah's face. Isabelle grabbed at the book, but as she did so, it fell from her hand and Aaron picked it up.

As Aaron looked wide-eyed at the book, Henry walked through the door, returning from a late-night meeting. "What's all the yelling? Why are your PJs wet, Sarah, have you been outside in the storm? Are you all right? Isabelle, Isabelle, why are you screaming at Sarah?"

"She has my book, the good--for--nothing"

"Will you stop! This is your flesh and blood child!"

Isabelle glared at Henry but sat down and said no more.

The room buzzed with a strident energy. Henry walked over to Isabelle to continue to berate his wife. "What do you think you are doing, talking to you daughter like this. Don't you know--"

Sarah put her hand on her dad's shoulder. "Leave Mum alone, Dad. Leave her alone! She is sorry."

Aaron raised his voice. "Shut up, everyone."

Henry sat down.

"I know the secret of the book. The book speaks to whoever is holding it, as long as we are together in the same room. I'm holding it now, so it's about me." He held up the book so his family could see the title. "Read the title, this is what the book is about. "The Language of Love." How can I know the meaning of these Latin words? I have no idea. Here it is:"

"Beware of Dragons. They come in many shapes and forms. They are not always playthings of the imagination. They may seem mischievous and fun-loving like you, but they shoot fire from their mouths and you can get burnt. Don't step too close. Find your Magic Circle. There will be no dragons there. Make up silly songs and use all the big words you want, as long as you understand their meanings. This is where wisdom begins. Love and cherish your sister, mother and father."

Everyone was silent. Aaron handed the book to his dad.

"Ahem, since we're all having a go. I'd like to say."

"Dad, you're not in a meeting, Read the book," Sarah interrupted.

"Ahem, yes—to begin."

"Dad, read!"

"A home is not just a set of designs and a few bits of wood, plaster and paint. You built this home. Spend some time in it with your family. Put down your briefcase. Stay for supper. Why does Sarah stand at the top of the driveway with tears in her eyes, watching you hit the mailbox as you back out every night? Because she loves you. Make her happy. Give her a joyful smile. And what about Aaron? Will he be only a singer of silly songs about dad missing supper, or can you teach him what you know about building and make him proud of you and you of him? Teach your wife how to be a good mother. She is long out of practice, and she is hollow and almost mad with loneliness. Find your family again."

No one spoke until Sarah broke the silence.

"The book was given to us as a sacred gift, to help unite us as a family. I love you all. Now, everyone get lost—out of my room all of you. Now!"

Infinito usually slept on the end of Sarah's bed, but tonight they slept wrapped around one another, content knowing that with the assistance of unseen powers, maybe even the horrible bird creature, they had helped their family. Sarah's last thought before sleeping was to ask herself, *why did the bird dragon bar me from the magic circle?*

The next day dawned bright and clear.

"Infinito, we need to find the raven, go to the clearing. I have a good feeling about today. Hopefully the dragon-bird has flown away. I'll bring the book. We can't wait for Aaron."

Infinito whined.

"Okay, you go and wake him up then."

In a flash Infinito jumped on top of Aaron, who was still sleeping in his bedroom next door

"Ohhh. What now?" Aaron sat up wiping sleep from his eyes. Then he remembered last night and guessed the rest. "Will you stop bouncing and licking my face. I'm coming. I'm coming."

In a few minutes the three were out the door and started down the wooded pathway at the end of the garden. Sarah guarded the book under her sweater.

When they reached the hollow tree where raven and babies had spent the night, Sarah poked her head inside the hole. It was empty. "I hope they weren't eaten by a fox. We should have left them in a safer place. But how could we do that in the storm?"

"Maybe they were eaten by a flesh-eating dragon with long sharp teeth and"

A knot formed in Sarah's throat, and she swallowed hard, remembering the creature in the pathway but determined to keep it to herself for now.

"Aaron," she spoke sharply. "I know more about dragons than you. They are real, like the book told you. Not just your imagination."

"For real, Sarah? How do you know about dragons?"

"I met one last night. He barred my path from the Magic Circle." *So much for keeping it to myself.* "It was part bird, I think."

"Serious? I'll never make up dragon stuff again. Holy fire-"

"Aaron—stop. Are you going to be of help here?"

"Yes, sorry. Infinito can sniff around for the raven's babies- I'll help him- but Sarah, you have to tell me more about the dragon?"

"Not now," she said, stepping quickly on ahead.

Infinito and Aaron ran ahead of Sarah, searching in the weeds and bushes. Aaron sang as he skipped along the path.

"Raven Mama, Call to us.
Messenger and Demon all in one.
Where do you hide, oh bird of black?
Speak to me and I'll speak back."

Sarah took a deep breath.

How does he do it? Aaron doesn't even know things for real, yet he does know inside, and it comes out in a song.

A few minutes later the raven answered, with a long, shrill caw from a tall pine tree.

"We found a nest. I'll meet you at the clearing later, if I can. Papa's away on business. Bringing food whenever he gets here. See you later. I am Rabein."

Papa's business, thought Sarah. *Sounds like our house. Glad they are all safe. How did Rabein know it would be alright to enter the clearing without another encounter with the dragon-bird? I am so glad, for Aaron's sake, but it is odd.*

When they reached the clearing, Narrito greeted them. "Salva, Sarah, Infinito ac Aaron."

"Salva, Narrito," Sarah replied, "I'm laetus superstites ultimum noctibus tempestas."

"I'm glad you are safe also, Sarah. Rabein the Raven looked after you last night, I hear."

"You're speaking English, Narrito- I don't understand."

"I can speak any language I wish. Your Latin is very good. How did you learn so quickly?"

"I don't know really. Many strange things are happening. I have been trying to speak Latin for you, but now you are speaking English. How odd is that?"

"Yes, many new things are happening to you and your family. I think life will begin to be better now. I must go, but I must to talk to Aaron first."

Aaron stood, looking up at Narrito. "Aaron, I hear you have been a fine, brave boy and smart enough now to know dragons can be real."

"Wow, thanks. Boy, you know about everything. You are really smart for a tree. How'd you know all this stuff?"

Sarah stepped back under the shelter of a nearby pine to listen to Aaron's conversation with Narrito. She saw the shadow within the tree smiling.

"I have been around a long time. When you are older, you will also be wise."

"I know you gave us the book so we could fix our family. Don't know if it will work, but we thank you for trying to help. We have come to give it back. I think we will all remember what was written to each of us, maybe even my mom and dad."

Infinito began whining and barking at Sarah, sniffing and poking his nose at her sweater.

"You want the book? What for?"

He whined again and scratched the earth.

"You want to bury it? What on earth?"

Narrito looked down on them, sadly.

Sarah looked up at Narrito to ask what to do, and he bowed his branches slightly towards the earth indicating - yes.

Infinito scratched at the earth again, right where he had dug up the book only days before. Aaron and Sarah stood solemnly by what felt to them like the book's grave. Then, as Infinito dug, his paws crunched against something hard. As he uncovered the object, Sarah could see it was a small, golden metal box with a tight-fitting lid. Infinito placed the book gently inside, closed the lid with his paw and covered the hole in with dirt.

I'm always wondering about the reasons for what happens. Maybe I don't always need to know everything all at once.

She looked up, expecting to see Narrito, but he had vanished. She thought she saw the man-shadow again, flittering between a distant row of scrubby trees.

"I guess we don't need him anymore," Sarah said sadly. "He's gone to help some other children."

"You got that right," squawked a voice from behind. "It's not the last you or Aaron will see of the book either."

"Rabein, you're here."

"Don't be upset. He has many lives, that old tree. More than a cat. Ohhh! What did I say? I hate to use that 'c' word. Let's go home, Sarah and Aaron."

Aaron ran ahead with the dog. Infinito sniffed ahead, along on the path.

"Let's go hunt for dragons, Infinito. I know for sure there's a real one around here somewhere. Sarah told me."

Infinito stopped at the base of a long pine. He looked up and a long wolf howl rang from deep inside.

"Glad you are our dog, Infinito. Sarah says you are smart. Now I know for sure."'

"Another question, Rabein, do you know anything about, well... a creature—kind of like a dragon with wings like a bird?"

"Dragon-birds, Sarah?" Rabein shook her feathers and looked down to the ground, as if she was scanning for bugs. "Maybe that's a question for another time. Like you say, you don't need to know all the reasons."

The two children and the dog said goodbye to Rabein at the bottom of her new tree home and promised to stay friends and meet up again soon. Then Rabein fluttered and flapped up to her nest to tend her babies.

When the children got home, Isabelle was outside digging in her flower beds. Sarah, expecting a tirade, tried to sneak by her mother.

"Sarah, can I ask for your help?"

Sarah thought she had heard wrong. *Her mother was asking for her help?*

Aaron went off around the house with his dad, who, surprisingly, was home on this sunny summer afternoon. "Aaron, would you like to see what I plan to do to upgrade the house?"

"Sure, Dad Holy Laughing Hyenas. Wow, Great."

"What did you say?"

"Oh nothing. Where are we going to start, Dad? Mom says the kitchen floor isn't level. I know lots of stuff."

Henry scratched his head and smiled down at Aaron. "Let's go look at the kitchen floor."

In the front garden, Isabelle asked Sarah, "I'm going to be teaching a three-day gardening course at the college, and I need to know the Latin names for some different flowers and bulbs. I've dug up a few bulbs here. Do you know the names of these ones?"

To her surprise, Sarah did know all the Latin names of the flowers and bulbs. In fact, from that day on, Sarah's understanding of Latin was nearly always perfect. Isabelle over time lost most of her facility with languages. She became more interested in her children's lives than her career and eventually resigned her job to become a stay-at-home mom. She gradually accepted this role and became a real guide and friend to her children. It helped that Henry also took more time off to work on upgrading the family home.

A week after she had helped identify the flower bulbs, Sarah went to town with her mother in the afternoon. They went to the library to check out some foreign- language books.

Isabelle told Sarah, "A daughter of mine, speaking Latin. I must say, I am proud, even though you didn't do anything to deserve it, really."

Sarah only smiled at her mother. "Maybe it's a gift."

While Isabelle was busy elsewhere, Sarah overheard a dark-haired girl about her age talking to the desk clerk and asking for a Latin-English dictionary. As she turned to leave Sarah noticed a bracelet the girl was wearing, made from what looked like silver, an infinity circle engraved on it.

Sarah approached the girl. "Hello, I couldn't help but notice you're wearing an interesting piece of silver jewellery. May I look at the inscription on your bracelet? I might be able to tell you what it says."

"Oh, would you?"

"May I?" Sarah took the bracelet in her hand.

Then she saw the word engraved inside one of the two infinity circles, as clearly as it had been engraved on the cover of the book.

"Infinito. The word means universal or infinite love. This locket must be very special to you."

"Oh, it is *very* special. It was given to me by my grandmother, who died recently. Thank you for translating. Are you crying? Do you want to sit down-what is it?"

"They are happy tears, very happy tears." Sarah smiled at the girl to reassure her. "Let's sit down."

They sat around the corner, away from the main stream of people.

"I'm Maria. My parents are originally from Italy. We just moved here from New York, and I'll be going to the local High School in September. And you?"

"I'm Sarah. I think we have a lot to talk about, Maria."

Sarah's head spun with new feelings and ideas.

Find your own magic circle, the book said. I think maybe I am finding my way.

"You know many other Latin words, Sarah?" Maria asked.

"Yes," She smiled wistfully at Maria. "It seems to come easily to me. Or maybe it's a gift."

Deanna Baran lives in Texas and is a librarian and former museum curator. She writes in between cups of tea and trading postcards with people around the world.

The Rishika of the Manika

By Deanna Baran

Five of us kids grew up in a three-bedroom bungalow. My parents had one bedroom, and the five of us crowded into the second bedroom, giving the shrine the third bedroom all to itself.

My family had guarded it for centuries. Originally, we had dwelled in the remote valleys of the Shivaliks but fled during times of political turmoil, when all the people were in danger of being murdered, pillaged, and burned. My great-great-grandfather was the one to abandon our traditional stronghold because he was the Rishi at the time, and no one else had the authority to make such a decision. We traveled around the globe, seeing where the shrine wanted to go, until it was clear its next permanent home would be in a humble little bungalow in a quiet neighbourhood. Then, it was given the honour of the third bedroom.

I wish the shrine had picked a bigger house. Maybe something with an extra bathroom, definitely something with a few more bedrooms. I love my four brothers, but as soon as I graduate from high school, I'm totally going to get a job and get my own apartment, just for some privacy.

If I became the Rishika, the bungalow would be mine. But I don't think that will happen, because it's been at least three centuries since the last time we had a female Rishika in our family. Usually, it's a male Rishi, and my father is the current one. He does the daily rituals in front of the shrine, and on the solstices and equinoxes, he opens it to conduct additional rites. All five of us help him—partly for safety, partly for community, and partly because we don't know who will succeed him as his heir, and it's important the rituals not be lost because we only taught the wrong person.

Four times a year, he brings out an enormous glowing ruby from the innermost compartment of the shrine. We call it the Manika. It's a legendary wish-fulfilling stone, which also allows you to read other people's souls. The catch, though, is that it doesn't work in this world, and you can't use it for yourself.

There are a thousand worlds out there besides ours, and the Rishi acts as a sort of benevolent deity for those worlds, even though he's an ordinary human in this world. He uses the power of the Manika to grant three wishes to the ruler of a troubled country who has conducted his own rituals. We use the solstices and the equinoxes to align the rituals in two different worlds, although I don't know whether that makes any sense. It would mean that the other worlds are all still somehow connected to Earth, right? Because otherwise, it wouldn't match. I tried having a scientific discussion with my father about it, about axial tilt and heliocentric longitude and stuff, but he just got annoyed and shut me down and told me that's how it was, so "don't overanalyze the supernatural from the material and physical perspective."

I still don't know if that was a real answer or if he was just trying to shut down my argument.

Today was the autumnal equinox, and the six of us were conducting our ceremony while my mother and grandmother cooked symbolic festival foods in the kitchen. I tried not to get distracted by the delicious smells. I chanted the words and rang

my bell, but my mind was elsewhere. The Manika needed to hurry up and choose the next Rishi. My twin elder brothers were beginning their senior year, but they couldn't apply to colleges without knowing whether one or both of them needed to stick around and serve the shrine on a daily basis. I was beginning my junior year, so I had a little more time. But for me, the danger was that if I was chosen, I'd have to marry someone from our clan to keep the knowledge of the Manika from leaking to outsiders. If I wasn't chosen, I could marry anyone I wanted. I wasn't really worried about it right now, because I had strict parents who made it clear that my job was to be a student and I was too young to date. But it was weird whenever I saw a guy I liked and imagined a relationship with him. Because it was always cool, until I got to the point in my fantasy where I had to break up with him and explain, "I'm sorry, I can't go out with you anymore, because I'm actually a benevolent deity for a mysterious kingdom."

Except, you don't get to explain.

I pulled my attention back to the ceremony. My father was getting to the part where he would pull out the Manika, and we would incense it and chant the purification rites. This was the key part, if the jewel-spirit was answering the prayers of an otherworldly king today, this was where something would happen.

My father carried the glowing ruby in its golden case. The incense curled, thick and fragrant. My two younger brothers beat their hand-drums; the rhythm pounded in my ears. I rang my bell at the right moments, a bright, clear brass note. The intensity was almost unbearable. Even though I kept up the chant with everyone else, I was holding my breath, waiting to see what would happen this time.

And what happened this time was that I could hear a far-off second wave of drums and bells and chanting, almost like people were playing the same song as us, but not quite matched. I wondered if it was a matter of distance because of the speed of sound. The nerdy part of my mind started trying to run the calculations, but I pushed that away and strained to listen.

The two rhythms separated a little, then came closer, then aligned.

When they matched just perfectly, a ruby glow filled my eyes and I could no longer see the third bedroom. When the glow cleared, I had the impression of lamps and carved statues and dozens of monks filling a soaring cavern with the urgency of their chanting, which had summoned me across time and space.

I locked eyes with their leader, who was offering incense at a small altar in front of me, standing closest to the dais on which I had manifested. He didn't look as surprised as I had imagined an otherworldly king might look upon the appearance of the Rishi, but he also definitely didn't look as though he was one hundred percent expecting me.

I wasn't expecting to be here, either. I'd never really considered myself, out of everyone in my bloodline, special enough to be chosen to carry on the work our clan had been doing for centuries. It was more responsibility than I'd ever handled, greater than studying for the PSAT's, greater than Junior Honor Society, greater than a 4.0 grade average.

And it would stick with me the rest of my life.

I stopped thinking about myself and turned my attention to the duty I'd been raised to keep in mind. First, I tried to analyze his appearance—probably not much older than my elder brothers, rich clothes, bareheaded, as good-looking as that guy on the soccer team who was in AP Chemistry with me—but I found myself getting distracted by this shimmering gold vapour behind him. As I focused on the vapour, it took the shape of some sort of attendant being. The being caught my eye and gave me a nod of acknowledgement but otherwise didn't do anything. I nodded back and looked more carefully at the other monks in the room, still kneeling and chanting and banging their drums and ringing their bells. There was gold vapour there as well. As I focused, other attendant beings manifested in all sorts of shapes and sizes.

I wished I could talk to them and ask what was going on. No one else paid any heed to their presence. I didn't know if that meant they were used to them, or if I was the only one who had eyes to see such things in this world. I brought my hand to my neck and found the Manika hanging there as a pendant, wondering if it was also still in the third bedroom back home, along with my real body.

By this point, others had become aware of my presence, and a collective gasp arose. Monks threw themselves face down on the floor. The music and chanting petered out as more and more men nose-dived to the ground.

Then there was nothing but silence.

Silence and expectation weighed heavily upon the air.

"I am the Rishika of the Manika. I bid you peace and greetings." That was safe.

The young king looked up at me. "Rishika, I bid you welcome. I am Nagitahra, Rajesh of Betwatama."

My mind worked furiously. Every time the Manika manifested its power, it was the responsibility of the Rishi to record the adventure and the responsibility of the future lineage to read and memorize the different histories and cultures. I couldn't remember anything about us working in Betwatama before. I wondered if the "Nagi" in "Nagitahra" implied that his kingdom worshipped snakes or crocodiles. I knew a Rajesh was a high king over lesser kings.

I hoped there wouldn't be snakes or crocodiles.

"The Rishika is only summoned in a time of crisis," I said. "The Manika has seen fit to consider your petitions. Let us retire somewhere more private."

"Yes, Your Holiness," Nagitahra said.

I descended from the dais with as much dignity as I could summon, but everyone seemed impressed anyway. We made a procession through the cavernous corridors—the monks, the king, me, and all of the shimmery golden spirit-beings.

Shortly afterward, I found myself in a luxurious apartment, simply but expensively furnished. There was a huge window with no glass but plenty of light and air—especially welcome after the lamplight struggling to fight back the darkness of the cavern. The Rajesh politely offered me refreshment, but I knew the answer to that already. The Rishika only ate and drank in total solitude, and I declined. He seemed pleased, and I had the feeling I had passed some sort of test.

As he spoke, I divided my attention between him and his golden spirit-attendant. His words were important in helping me figure out what was going on, but his spirit-attendant was churning and roiling at its centre in a very distracting way.

"As I'm sure you know, Betwatama is a confederation of smaller kingdoms," he explained. "All of us rulers are kin in one way or another, although there are twelve main bloodlines. Sometimes, one of the bloodlines may be the most powerful, and other years, another bloodline may reach ascendancy, but in general, there are twelve families ruling over thirty-two smaller kingdoms. At the death of each Rajesh, the twelve families meet and the next Rajesh is elected." He looked at me. "I have been Rajesh for fifteen years already."

I stifled a gasp and ran the math through my head. That must mean Nagitahra had only been a child of four or five when he was originally elected. And *that* must mean he had been someone's puppet for a long time. And the fact I had been summoned must mean he was rebelling against the puppet-master and events were beginning to cascade out of control.

"My father preceded me as Rajesh, but was assassinated when I was very young," he said. "My family had only recently gained ascendancy and did not wish to lose control after only one rule. He had three brothers. None of the three brothers had sufficient support to become the next Rajesh. I was the compromise, and the three brothers ruled in my name as co-regents. Until recently."

"And recently?" I asked, encouraging him to go on.

"Recently, there have been accidents," Nagitahra said. "One of my uncles died in a hunting accident. I myself have avoided death five times in the last three months. I do not know if I am to trust one, both, or neither of my uncles. I need guidance."

"Is that your first wish?" I asked him.

"I want to bring you all my ministers. Read their hearts. Root out the corruption. There is too much evil. They all smile to my face, and I no longer trust my own judgment in distinguishing between the faithful and the treacherous."

I frowned. "Is that really wise?" I asked him, casting my mind back to one particular adventure during my sixth-great grandfather's time. "Virtue is important, I agree, but what would a country be like if it was run solely with mercy? Utopias only work in fiction; they're not compatible with human nature. Sometimes we do our best with imperfect people. Not everyone who's bad in one way is necessarily bad in all ways."

Nagitahra looked at me with something like a sneer. Puppet king though he was and benevolent deity though I was supposed to be, he obviously wasn't used to having to defend his position. "My first wish is my first wish," he said imperiously. "I shall present each of my ministers. You shall read their hearts and indicate to me their faults."

I closed my eyes and tried to calm my racing heart. I had no doubt there was about to be a great amount of death and bloodshed, and there would be more job openings than he intended. In the case of an active assassination attempt, yeah, I could understand his stubbornness and his paranoia. But the way he had phrased things, he was probably going to end up very, very vulnerable.

One of the first things we learn is that it's good we don't get what we deserve in this lifetime.

I could see the glow of the Manika through my eyelids as it began its work. My opinion of the wish didn't mean anything; I was ultimately just as much a puppet as he was. "Rajesh of Betwatama, the Manika grants your first wish," I said solemnly, but my eyes gazed beyond him at the golden entity. A mutual feeling of sorrow passed silently between us. Whatever this led to, we both knew it wouldn't solve the churning at its core. "Make the arrangements."

Shortly afterward, I was ensconced atop the dais once more, with the Rajesh enthroned by my feet, within whispering distance. I didn't quite know how this reading-of-hearts thing was supposed to go, but I figured the Manika would take care of it as it always did. The worst that could happen would be the Manika remaining silent on the subject, and providing no information, and the wish would be wasted.

But the Manika worked, as it always does, and I dutifully relayed to Nagitahra the information he sought regarding his court.

We started in the lower ranks, working our way up.

The first to offer incense and prostrate themselves for my scrutiny were the four Ministers of Civil Administration.

It was very obvious from the first that I was not to look closely at the humans but at their golden spirit-attendants. If I had to explain it, they were kind of like visual metaphors for a spiritual reality. One of the first things we're taught in shrine service is that there are three realms: the physical, the spiritual, and the soul-realm. The physical is where stuff like the shrine or the ruby exist. The spiritual is where things like the deity behind the Manika exist. And the soul-realm is where our thoughts and decisions exist. All three realms are tightly tied to each other and constantly affect each other, so that a decision in the soul-realm to do a good deed in the physical realm leads to merit in the spiritual realm. And likewise, a decision in the soul-realm to do a bad deed in the physical realm leads to disadvantage in the spirit-realm. So these golden attendants were manifestations of a lifetime of good work or a lifetime of error. But most often, they were a combination of both, because humans naturally have their virtues and their flaws—few people are ever entirely virtuous, and few people are ever entirely flawed.

Especially in a royal court.

As I made the connections between what I was seeing, I felt embarrassed, as though I was intruding on someone's privacy far more intimately than sharing a room with four brothers had ever intruded on mine. I was looking into the depths of their souls and matter-of-factly whispering all of their innermost weaknesses to their high king. The sorts of secrets that you hide from everyone, even yourself.

It's not the sort of scrutiny I'd ever want to subject myself to.

And as I spoke, I watched Nagitahra's own golden attendant. When I first saw it, it had been tall and proud, like a powerful golden warrior capable of great achievements, but even then its centre had been a churning mass of insecurities that would cripple it if they took over. Now it greedily devoured all the private information I could feed it. The more it feasted upon knowledge of the ministers' and courtiers' weaknesses, the less it looked like a tall, proud warrior and the more it looked like a greedy monstrosity. Its impressive royal power, instead of focusing on being a confident ruler amidst challenging circumstances, was feeding upon all the petty fears and festering vindictiveness Nagitahra had stored up over his entire lifetime and was now wallowing in the revelations of others' flaws.

I felt sorry for it, and I felt sorry for the people of Betwatama. Surely, they deserved better than this.

We made our way through the Four Ministers of Ceremonies, the Four Ministers of Popular Affairs, the Four Ministers of Central Affairs, the Four Ministers of War, the Four Ministers of Justice, the Four Ministers of the Treasury, and the Four Ministers of the Royal Household. We made our way up to the Junior Recorders and the Senior Recorders; the Minor, Middle, and Major Controllers; the Three Ministers; the two Great Ministers; the Controlling Board; the Great Council of State; and the Two Ex-Regents.

There was the usual mix of greed, ambition, pride, egotism, hubris, envy. In large quantities. You find it in any group of people who remorselessly pursue power and influence regardless of the cost. Being forced to focus on it made me sick. But it wasn't just cartoonish bad-guy stuff, even though I saw the spiritual leftovers of countless truly reprehensible deeds. There were also large quantities of fear. Of wishing to please others with their success. Of being driven and encouraged to do wrong by family members, friends, and loved ones, who were happy to ignore the evil and focus only on the benefit. Of driving others to do bad deeds on their behalf and not realizing that the poison would corrode themselves as well, even if their hands were technically clean.

Neither of the two uncles were anything near virtuous, in case you were wondering. I described their crimes just as remorselessly as I had everyone else's. I pointed out which one was in cahoots with the Captain of the Bodyguard and mentioned how much he had paid to relax the usual security protocols for three of the assassination attempts. Then I pointed out which one had been in cahoots with the Tansaq family, who had proof he had been stealing from the treasury and were holding it over him in exchange for his cooperation in toppling the current dynasty. The first step had involved the murder of his brother, and the second step had been the other two attempts on the life of the current Rajesh.

Nagitahra looked exultant as the last of the Court was escorted from the chamber. I knew a good number of them would not survive to see the next dawn, and I tried hard not to think about that. Ugly stuff like this happened all the time in the archives, but I'd always thought of it in a very abstract way, like a math problem or a history question, rather than something that had been lived by real people. The Manika didn't make mistakes, so I was confident in my facts, but that didn't keep my stomach from knotting up, knowing that I was the one sending those sons, husbands, and fathers off to their deaths. I'd always looked forward to the idea of making a difference with my timely magic wishes; it never occurred to me that I would be responsible for distributing large quantities of death. It still hadn't totally sunk in, but a wave of nausea was already present and my arms and legs felt as weak as noodles.

"Rishika of the Manika," Nagitahra said, standing up and inclining his head in as close to a respectful bow as he ever got, "heed my second wish."

I couldn't tell him I just wanted some food and a nap. How much time had passed? I knew from the records that almost no time would have passed once I got home, but my stomach would be starving once I'd emotionally processed everything I'd been through this far. And after I took something for the nausea.

"Nagitahra, Rajesh of Betwatama, speak, for I listen," I said formally.

"The Queen of Dabqa is legendary for her beauty," he said. "And she is equally legendary for her wealth. She controls the realms of twelve minor kings by her own hand. She toys with princes and kings and emperors, who all hope to marry her and acquire her beauty and her wealth for themselves. But she knows that her political power is in never committing to unity with one man, for as soon as she expresses a definite choice, she is locked into the alliances and enemies that come with him. I grow weary of this game. My second wish is for you to bring the Queen of Dabqa here, so that Betwatama and Dabqa may unite."

Another frown crossed my face. I didn't want to argue with him in front of the few courtiers and soldiers who were left inside the great vaulted chamber, but I took the chance. "That's not a good idea," I murmured. "Even the great Manika cannot change hearts. It cannot make her love you if she does not already do so. Do you desire her beauty and her wealth so much that you would risk her hatred?"

Nagitahra looked at me as though I was the most annoying insect on the planet. "My second wish is for you to bring the High Queen of Dabqa here, so that Betwatama and Dabqa may unite," he repeated, hissing the words through clenched teeth.

I glanced at the roiling golden spirit. It wasn't merely churning like gangbusters; the internal colours had taken on a shadowy appearance.

This wasn't healthy for him. Out of all the virtuous kings out there this autumn, why couldn't the Manika have chosen a nice guy in trouble?

"Rajesh of Betwatama, the Manika grants your second wish," I said as neutrally as I could. I raised my arm because it felt right, and there was a great flash of red light.

A tall, proud-looking woman stood in the middle of the cavern. Her hair was a bit of a mess and it seemed she had been in the process of getting ready for bed, because she was wearing thin, elegant under-robes, not the over-robes that you would expect a queen to wear. I wondered if this was this world's equivalent of zapping someone somewhere in just their underwear. Although she was surprised, her regal upbringing kicked in, and she coolly demanded to know what was going on.

"I am Nagitahra, Rajesh of Betwatama." He had obviously expected his wish to be granted, but I think both of us were a little surprised at the promptness with which it had happened. He stood up and made a courteous bow—conveying more respect than he had shown me to date, goshdarnit, and I was supposed to be a benevolent deity. "Dearest Devika, Rajeshka of Dabqa. Heaven has smiled upon us. I have long admired you and sought your hand. My powerful magicians have brought you here, for our marriage and the unity of our kingdoms."

Her eyes narrowed. She was no inexperienced girl. She wasn't old enough to be his mother but clearly had enough experience to not be flattered by that kind of speech.

"Then have your powerful magicians send me home, for I have no intention of marrying you or unifying our kingdoms," she said coldly.

Nagitahra was obviously expecting a different reaction, although I don't know why. He seemed offended, and perhaps a little humiliated in front of the remnants of his court. "How unlike you," he sneered. "You don't always speak so straightforwardly. Usually you leave just enough hope alight in the hearts of your suitors that none of them go away completely without optimism."

Devika looked like she was quickly realizing she was speaking with a crazy man. She looked a little fascinated, a little repulsed, and more than a little offended. But she responded, "It is my rule that I will never marry a kidnapper."

Nagitahra gave her the sneer that he usually reserved for me. "I have some very comfortable apartments prepared for you," he said. "Perhaps, if you have a little time to think it over, you will be able to appreciate my suit in its proper light." A subtle gesture, and six armed warriors approached her. (The reading-of-the-heart business, fortunately, hadn't eliminated the entire palace guard.) Devika looked scornfully at their drawn weapons, lifted her head proudly, and regally exited the room along the indicated path.

I watched with a great sense of unease. Her golden spirit was proud and noble, doing a good job of hiding insecurity and loneliness. I didn't want any of these events to damage it like Nagitahra's was getting corrupted the longer I stayed.

"I suppose you'll have to think over your third and final wish," I said feebly, hoping he would give me a little privacy to eat, drink, and rest. I was merely the puppet of the Manika, but I was exhausted by this point.

"I don't need to think about my third and final wish," said Nagitahra, his eyes fixed on where the Rajeshka had exited. "I already know what I wish."

I looked at him doubtfully. His reign was in crisis, for sure. I didn't know much about the politics and policies of his government, but I suspected it wasn't doing so great at this point either. None of his wishes were doing anything to really improve the roots of his trouble. He had not only just weakened his government by leaving a great vacuum through the wholesale purge of flawed and powerful men, but obviously never read *The Iliad*. That's where Paris had abducted Helen after she'd married Menelaus, and all the other rejected suitors had agreed to defend the man Helen had chosen. And Devika hadn't chosen anyone. But I suspected that as soon as word leaked out that Nagitahra had abducted Devika, all the other would-be suitors would use it as a great excuse to ravage the thirty-two kingdoms of Betwatama.

But heck. I'm just a junior in high school. What do I know about international politics?

"Speak, Rajesh of Betwatama."

"She thinks so little of me because I'm not as rich as the Rajesh of Dholba, or as handsome as the Rajah of Mahabasu, or a great warrior king like Aurangaza the Conqueror," he seethed. "My third wish—"

I saw where this was going, and I interrupted him because that's what a benevolent god does when they see someone about to be foolish a third time.

"You know yourself that she has her own reasons for encouraging suitors yet never actually making a choice," I said. "So why not look to someone who actually is interested in marrying a king? Someone who wants to be on your team. Someone who wants to help fix your country and make it into a splendid place. Someone who can contribute to something good you build together. Not someone who you've brought here against her will, someone who you'll marry against her will, and someone who will be kept here against her will. You want her land and her riches, but if you have to hide her and fight her, how in the world will you lay claim to them anyways? That doesn't make sense. And that's totally ignoring the fact that I don't even think you're able to marry someone without her consent. Force and duress and coercion make it voidable, right?"

He let me finish but glared at me the entire time I spoke. "My third and final wish, O Rishika of the Manika," he said, "is for me to acquire wealth ten times greater than that of the Rajesh of Dholba, good looks ten times superior to those of the Rajah of Mahabasu, and strength and strategy ten times superior to that of Aurangaza the Conqueror."

I wasn't sure if that counted as a single wish or if the Manika would interpret that as three separate wishes and therefore a no-go, but there was the flash of red before either of us could start a fresh argument.

The vast chamber flooded with gold coins like something out of Scrooge McDuck's vault. It reminded me of one African king I'd read about in world history who'd given away so much gold while on pilgrimage to Mecca that it totally wrecked the economies of the countries he'd traveled through for the next twenty years.

I have no clue what the Rajah of Mahabasu looked like, but Nagitahra now looked way handsomer than that guy on the soccer team in AP Chemistry. He even looked better than the guy in that movie that all the girls in Student Council had gushed over for a week. And yet, no matter how handsome his features were, I could still see his golden spirit, which was growing more and more warped and bestial. The fear and uncertainty had tainted it before, but that fear and uncertainty were better than what was in control now. I turned my face away.

Seeing that his wealth had instantly increased into the bazillions, and his good looks had increased as well, I presumed that the Manika had also taken care of his strength and strategy. His clothes provided too much coverage for me to really analyze his physique, but it definitely wasn't like the overdeveloped guys on steroids you see in the bodybuilding magazines.

Thank goodness for that, Manika.

I wondered if his increased sense of strategy would pick up on the trap that he had laid himself and was in the process of walking into.

But I wasn't about to find out because as he turned to speak to me, there was a flash of red. I closed my eyes to keep from being blinded by the ruby brightness, and when I opened them again, there I was on the divan in the third bedroom with my father and brothers and mother and grandmother all looking anxiously at me.

I sat up and I cried.

My father took me into his arms, and I sobbed into his neck. I figured he, of all people, ought to understand.

"It didn't make anything better," I sobbed. "It only made things worse."

When I had imagined myself as Rishika, I had always envisioned myself as a magic genie, coming in to save the day with my magic powers. I'd work with a wise and benevolent ruler who would correct his country's path, and they would go on for another thousand years of peaceful rule. I had never envisioned working for someone who was greedy, selfish, petty, and small-minded, who would squander his three wishes on stupid stuff like, "Make someone marry me who obviously doesn't want to," or "Make me rich and good-looking so she'll overlook my emptiness."

"That's how it is sometimes, especially in autumn and winter," my father said, petting my hair and letting me cry. He gave me a cloth dinner napkin, and I blew my nose loudly. "Think back to the archives and what has happened before. In order to know how your story ends, we need to recognize the pattern. What do you think will happen?"

I sketched out the events as best I could. "So the families will probably turn on Nagitahra, because you know anyone he purges is going to be a powerful individual from a powerful family," I concluded. "That will weaken his support at home. The ones who remain, even if they were content with him before, will definitely rise up against him in one way or another. At the same time, the secret's going to get out that Devika is captive against her will. That's not the sort of thing that will be overlooked, especially since he wasn't merely content with possessing her physically but wanted to acquire her land and her treasure as well. With all the gold he got with his third wish, I don't know if her wealth is an issue anymore, but the power from increasing the number of kingdoms under his control from thirty-two to, um, forty-four, is definitely significant. I don't know what his strategy is for getting her twelve kingdoms under his thumb, especially with her lack of cooperation, but being such a great strategist, I figure he has some sort of reasoning."

"He made the strategy before he became a great strategist," my father pointed out. "I wouldn't count on it."

"True. So either he has a half-baked plan that will fail, or he realizes he has a half-baked plan and replaces it with something better, but he still doesn't have the support he needs to carry it off with a high likelihood of success," I agreed. "And with that ridiculous amount of gold he got at the very end, I have no doubt people will be squabbling over control of his country and his treasure for a century after his death."

My father nodded. "It will be ravaged. And then perhaps something worthwhile will rise from the ashes of his destruction. It's part of the cycle. Life and death. Birth and rebirth. All civilizations go through it. And sometimes, it's our job to help. Not everything that is broken can be mended.

Sometimes, things need to start over, and we hope to avoid the mistakes that led to the brokenness in the first place."

"That's a lot to think about," I mused. Then my stomach growled, and I winced with embarrassment. "Can I think about it while we eat? I'm starved."

A successful forty plus year career as a self-employed building contractor has afforded Byrne Montgomery the freedom to pursue his greatest passion—to travel the world. These travels have inspired him to write stories and poems about the many places he's visited.

It is not, however, only the sights, sounds and smells—the cultural mosaic—of these places that inspire him. It is the intriguing tales told by fellow travellers he's met along his journeys that interest him the most.

While in Singapore in 2004, Mr. Montgomery began writing a full-length crime novel. Ten years and hundreds of gruelling hours later he proudly self-published the book to a 60-70 percent "thumbs-up".

His story in Mythical Girls— "A Princess, A Comb and a Young Girl" is based on an actual village in Myanmar and on a legend that still exists to this day.

A Princess, a Comb, and a Young Girl

(Mainnsamee, Bhee, Nhang Ngaairwal Meinkalayy)

By Byrne Montgomery

Achara had few friends. The girls at school were polite to her face, but she heard their whispers behind her back. "Her mother is dead and her father ran off when she was born," or "She's not really Burmese you know," or "A Burmese mother and Thai father makes her a foreigner."

But the worst was how they made her out to be a peasant.

"Look at her threadbare clothes and tattered shoes. I hear she begs on the streets for food."

Her mother, who had died shortly after Achara's birth, was a local Bwe Kayin girl from the Burmese village of Thandauan, who, against local customs, dared to marry a foreigner—a Thai man she dearly loved. The truth? He had *not* run off. Devastated by his young bride's unexpected death, he'd become a Bhikku—a monk dedicated to a lifelong devotion to Buddhism. And although he lived in a remote monastery in northern Thailand, he somehow managed the annual arduous barefoot journey to attend Achara's birthday celebration—the last being her tenth.

She however had to agree with her tormentors' assessment of her clothing. Yes, it was threadbare. Her grandfather, whom she lived with, was a simple tea farmer with little income and each item of clothing was simply worn until it was worn out.

But the cruel comments about her begging for food? Nothing could have been farther from the truth. Although she never heeded their whispers, her answer would have been, "Grandfather is a shrewd businessman. He trades his tea for all the food we need. I *never* go to bed hungry."

She truly believed their cruel comments were born out of envy—resentment that she had a pet they could only dream to having—a full-grown male Indochinese tiger. After poachers had killed the mother tiger and left her cub to die, her grandfather found him at death's door, nursed him back to health, and lovingly raised him as part of the family.

Achara was too young to remember when Shadow had first arrived but could fondly remember them growing up together and becoming best buds.

It's not that important to have a lot of friends, she often thought. *Between homework and chores, where would I have the time to hang out with friends? I hope to be a teacher someday and I'll stress to my students that those that have less possessions are not lesser human beings. Doesn't Buddha preach it is those who have enough, but not too much, who are the happiest?*

Daily, as Achara returned from school, Shadow, without fail, would be waiting at their pathway for her. Together, they would chase butterflies through the meadows. At night, he slept curled up on the floor at her feet. "Inseparable" was the word the villagers used to describe them.

On one such romp through the grasslands, as she sat beside a stream to catch her breath, Achara noticed Shadow pawing at the water's edge. Something he'd unearthed glinted in the bright sunshine. Hoping it was coins someone had mistakenly dropped, she discovered it wasn't something of value as she'd wished. The object was a large shiny silver comb.

Almost as long as her hand, it had an "old" look to it—more of a feel of old than actual look. Cool to the touch, each time after running her fingers down its length, Achara was left with a slight dizziness—and thoughts of cold. "Wha...? Strange. What does cold look like, Shadow?" she asked her furry companion.

Thoughts and feelings from a simple touch? Odd, to say the least. I'll show Grandfather what we've found. Surely, he will know what it is.

As she ran her fingers once more down the comb's length, it perplexed her how she could feel a sinister chill emanating from its surface.

After she'd stuffed the comb into her backpack, she said, "We'd better get going Shadow. We have butterflies to chase and chores to do before dinnertime."

By the time they'd arrived home, Achara had completely forgotten the comb and her intentions to query her grandfather about it.

Most nights, at bedtime, Achara's grandfather would tell her a bedtime story he himself had heard as a boy—either a story of Buddha's life, beliefs or teachings, or one of the local fables. *Grandfather is the smartest person I know. I'm sure he's wiser than any of my teachers or schoolmates. He probably knows more about Buddha than all the monks at the temple combined.*

After the bedtime story it was customarily lights out with no more talking. But on this occasion, Achara persisted with a question. "Pho (grandfather), who is more powerful, Mother Earth or Buddha himself?"

Grandfather sat in silence for longer than she could remember. The unanswered question hung thickly in the air.

Achara was well aware the word "hurry" was buried deep beneath this gentle and wrinkled old soul's skin. Many times, at the market, she had observed how the vendors would push Grandfather to make his offer, but to no avail. She dared not interrupt for fear of a reprimand. Grandfather's internal clock ran much slower than the one on her school's wall.

With his usual patience and mindfulness, Grandfather finally answered her philosophical question with a single word. "Meditation." In a heartbeat, Achara knew what *that* meant. After school (upon completion of her chores) grandfather would trudge with her up the mountainside to their favourite lookout. Here they would sit side-by-side in lotus position and meditate until after dark.

Achara relished these treks. Not only because of her "together-time" with this wise old soul but she would invariably be given a sweet treat on their way home. And on occasion, the sweet would be a piece of chocolate—her favourite.

***

Upon arriving at the cliffside lookout her grandfather again stressed, "Achara, you must concentrate wholly on your breathing—in through your nose and exhale through your mouth. If your mind wanders, remove the thoughts and gently focus again on your breath. Proper meditation takes great practice. But I promise, once you have mastered it, with inner peace comes the answers to many questions."

This breathtaking vantage point always made it difficult for her to concentrate. Far below, as both the evening lights of Thandauan twinkled alive and the familiar sound of the big brass bell in the town's centre (rung every evening at sunset) echoed up to them, her mind wandered.

Sorry Grandfather. It is difficult for me to clear my mind of all thought.

Although she knew little about the outside world other than from picture books, Achara loved where she lived—it was paradise to her. As far as she could see, the mountains and valleys were covered in ancient twisted trees, thick with climbing vines. Sparkling streams snaked throughout the valley bottoms. Wildflowers grew everywhere—their smells almost overwhelming. Most of the townsfolk had farm animals and pets; with few tied or penned up. The many dogs, cats, chickens, geese, cows, and ducks all lived in harmony.

Achara did, however, worry about the earthquakes and landslides that often racked the area. In her few years on this earth she had only felt a dozen or so violent tremors, but from both her schoolteachers' and grandfather's accounts, devastation had happened before and could happen again at any time.

She could not imagine such beauty being reduced to rubble.

Surely Mother Nature could not be that cruel. But what would I do if such a catastrophe hit? Where would I go? Could I be of any help to those in distress?

Upon her remembering the comb still in her backpack and a furtive glance at her grandfather's closed eyes, she thought, *I'll pull my hair back with it and see if Grandfather notices.*

The instant she slid the silver comb into her long black locks, she found herself—dreamlike—high in the sky peering down at the ground through the eyes of a soaring eagle.

Through its eyes, she could see the ground with amazing clarity. The dizzying height took her breath away. The sensation of free flight engulfed her entire being.

Her inner smile was disrupted by an overwhelming urgency compelling her to identify something far below on the ground.

Intently, she peered through her eagle eyes; but before she could determine what it was, she woke up with a start.

On the ground and once again herself, she was not frightened by this bizarre happening. A calmness radiated throughout her.

Achara wanted to ask Grandfather about the significance of such a daydream. But as per their arrangement, only after the sun (now a fiery ball sliding below the horizon) had set, was she allowed to talk. She furtively removed the comb from her hair and replaced it in her backpack.

She decided to honour his wish for silence. Out of respect, she would at least pretend to meditate and save that question for bedtime.

That evening, snug in her woolen blanket and Shadow asleep at her feet, with confidence she said, "Pho, I believe I can answer the question I asked earlier. Neither is more powerful. Buddha is Mother Earth and Mother Earth is Buddha. Am I right?"

"You are wise beyond your years, little bird," he answered. "But as our great leader once taught, 'Three things cannot be long hidden: the sun, the moon, and the truth'.

"The truth? As great as he was, Buddha was only a part of this world and unable to influence Mother Nature in any way. Her decisions are hers, and hers alone. Mother Nature is much bigger than we can imagine. She is the stars, the planets—all of the universe combined."

Achara loved her grandfather's pet name for her—"hnget" (little bird). With her heart full of adoration, she decided to not burden him with any additional questions.

The eagle dream was merely a fantasy—I'll ask him about it another time.

But had she asked, she might have been told the connection between the soaring eagle daydream and something that had happened to her grandfather as a young boy.

For weeks, the comb lay forgotten at the bottom of her backpack.

***

On non-school days, Achara and Shadow would hike high into the mountain meadows looking for adventure. If darkness fell upon them, seldom would her grandfather worry about them. Any strangers they encountered, upon eyeing the huge, wild beast at the girl's side, would invariably run away in fear.

And although Shadow was a natural-born hunter with an instinctive taste for meat, he never chased any of the wildlife they often came face-to-face with. At worst, his eyes would narrow and the fur on his neck would stand on end but immediately relax upon hearing, in Achara's soothing tone, "Easy, Shadow, don't worry, Grandfather will feed you when we get home."

On one such hiking trip, something happened of such magnitude it would forever change Achara's life as she knew it.

At daybreak—with a clear sky, crisp air, and her backpack stuffed at Grandfather's insistence, with a prepared lunch of sticky rice and water, and a few emergency supplies: a candle, matches and a few bandages—the two struck out on their journey. Achara was filled with anticipation. A full day of fun and adventure lay before them.

High up the mountainside they trekked. As they came upon her grandfather's favourite meditation lookout, Achara remembered the comb, still tucked in her backpack. As she nervously glided it into her hair, she was again, in a flash, transformed into the soaring eagle—earnestly scanning the earth through its eyes. In that instant, the object she previously had not been able to make out now came into focus. A beautiful blond-haired lady was smiling up at her.

Something was telling Achara she knew who this lady was, but the unsettling feeling that this was reality, not fantasy, frightened her. She tore the comb from her hair and jolted out of her reverie with a start.

Shadow jumped from her side and stared back at her, his eyes clouded with confusion, his neck hair standing at attention.

"Oh Shadow, I am so sorry I frightened you," she said as she patted down his neck fur. "There is nothing to be afraid of. I was merely having a daydream."

She tried to convince herself that was what had just happened, but her heart told her this weird experience was more than a simple daydream.

Her explanation to Shadow did not dull the uneasiness she felt. To soothe her jumpy nerves, she hugged her furry friend. "Come on Shadow, let's get on with our hike—adventure lies ahead."

As they trekked on, Achara tried to convince herself that all was well in the world, but there was this underlying feeling of ...of...what? Was something bad about to happen? No...it was more than that. Impending doom? Yes! That was exactly the message she was sensing. And she was sure the lovely maiden she had spied from high in the sky had something to do with these unsettling premonitions. Not the maiden's presence in itself—she sensed a kinship of sorts with her— but...but what?

***

As the two buds trudged up the sunny side of Naw Bu Baw Mountain, Achara's spirits lifted, and in minutes, any apprehensions she had previously harboured were forgotten—her concentration now focused on the direction they should take.

The path she'd chosen ended at the base of a sheer rock wall. To both the left and right, lay a labyrinth of vines and fallen trees.

"It's too early to head for home, Shadow. Let's see if we can find a way around this cliff."

After an hour or so of arduous clambering over and under a jungle of fallen boughs and vines, Achara decided enough was enough. "I'm sorry, Shadow, but adventure does not seem too probable today, ol' friend. If we head back to the path now, we can be home before dark."

No sooner had she spoken these words than a thick, wet fog enveloped them. Achara could not determine which direction to take. A chill ran up her spine.

Grandfather had cautioned her not to venture too far up the mountainside. He'd warned her the weather patterns in these hills were unstable. Hikers, he claimed, were often stranded in the middle of a storm or enshrouded in thick mist with visibility reduced to an arm's length.

Stumbling blindly through the tangled jungle, wet and exhausted, with both hands and knees scraped and bleeding, Achara sat on a fallen tree to rest. Panic swelled within her.

Not weak of heart, she resolved that bemoaning her situation would not solve her dilemma. She would get herself and her furry companion safely home. Period!

Shadow, alerted by something, softly growled. His intent stare focused straight ahead.

"What are you staring at?" Achara asked. A shiver, again, ran up her spine. "How can see anything through this foggy pea soup? What is it, Shadow? What...what...?"

In that instant, she could see what had caught his attention. A bright shimmering light in the shape of a human peeked back at them through the fog.

"Hello, hello...is anybody there." she nervously hollered. No response. But as she again yelled, "Hello! Can you see us?" the human-like light seemed to beckon for them to follow.

Why Achara felt the need to follow something so out of the ordinary, she could not explain. It was merely a feeling. Not a sense of danger, more a feeling of serenity.

The apparition led them back to a well-beaten path, making their attempt to catch up to the light much easier. And although they seemed to never get any closer to the luminescence, Achara felt an internal calmness similar to the tranquility she felt when Grandfather recounted his bedtime tales to her.

In the blink of an eye, they were again left in murkiness. Achara, although baffled by this strange happening, presumed her imagination was playing tricks on her. "It's merely the town's lights reflecting off the fog bank, Shadow," she rationalized.

Disappointed and about to turn around, the light reappeared, and she could clearly see *someone* was in the light. The shimmering apparition was beckoning for them to follow it into a cave entrance.

Risk, she had learned from Grandfather, was never the best option. *How had he put it?* she thought. *Oh, yes, "Discretion is the better part of valour." Entering this cave without knowing what to expect is not using discretion? Does danger lie waiting*?

Achara studied Shadow's neck fur. Not one hair stood on end. He was neither walking close to the ground nor quietly growling—his instinctual reaction when danger lurked close by.

But hadn't Grandfather also claimed, "Curiosity killed the cat?" She giggled.

Her decision did not take long. With her mind made up, she followed the apparition into the cave. Prudently, she let Shadow lead the way.

The cave portal was smaller than expected. Forced to crawl on her scraped hands and knees, she barely managed to squeeze through the narrow opening.

To her amazement, once inside, a mighty cavern lit by hundreds of candles encompassed them. The previous feeling of serenity again cloaked her in comfort.

The ghost-like image gestured them to follow it down a steep stairway carved in the stone floor. But before she could say, "Wait for me, I'm coming with you," Shadow had disappeared down the stairs.

Where the stairs ended, they perched on a stone ledge high above a vast lake with water almost transparent, Achara stood in awe. The colossal cavern walls shimmered in a soft golden glow.

The lake's surface began to swirl, forming a deep whirlpool.

From the centre of this twisting translucence, an enormous seashell rose. In its centre, on a silver throne, sat a beautiful lady in a full-length white gown. Her blond hair shone as bright as the sun.

Achara, still wonderstruck, boldly cried out, "I know you! You're the lady I saw from high in the sky." Regretful she had said *anything* to the goddess, she bit her lip to rein in her enthusiasm.

In a resounding voice of liquid gold came the response, "Yes, it is I you saw smiling up at you as you soared high above the earth. That was not a dream as you thought, but something I have planned for you since your Grandfather was a young boy.

"Pray tell, Achara, have you heard the legend of Naw Bu Baw and her handsome prince Saw Thaw oh Khwa?" the lady asked.

"Yes, we were taught the legend in school, but I thought it was merely a fairytale—"

"No, child," the princess interrupted, "it is not a fairytale. Let me tell you the real truth of what happened eons ago.

"Crossing the ocean, Saw Thaw, the son of King Kiku of these highlands was en route to battle enemy armies. His boat sank in a violent storm. I am Naw Bu Baw, the daughter of the king of the sea. Similar to a dolphin, I am a powerful swimmer, and after I had saved him from drowning, we fell in love. I believe you humans call it 'love at first sight.'

"As newlyweds, we returned to these mountains and scoured the hills and meadows, hand in hand, in search of a perfect setting in which to build our castle. However, the local Kayin people did not accept me. It was not because of my blond hair or fair skin. They believed I was not worthy of Prince Thaw. And because of the powers of my silver comb—a magical comb that when I put it under my feet, made me invisible—I was labelled an evil sorceress.

"One day Prince Thaw was asked by his father to lead an army into the Eastern mountains to repel invading enemies. I presented my husband with the magical comb to enable him to safely disappear when his enemies attacked.

"One of my powers I never revealed to anyone, even to my prince, is my ability to transform into any animal or sea creature. As an eagle I followed him into battle with the hopes of warning him of impending danger. What I did not know was that in a man's hand, the comb's power is useless. Defenseless, he died on the battlefield. The locals here, distraught and angry, blamed me for his death. In hopes that evil spirits would eventually devour me, they imprisoned me in this rock cavern. Little did they know, I can leave at any time—but only as an eagle or an apparition as you now know.

"And that, Achara, is the truth to the legend.

"However," the princess stressed, "the legend has little to do with you being here now. You are here for a reason. Something I have planned since your grandfather was a young boy...."

"Grandfather!" Achara interrupted, "What has Grandfather got to do with—" The princess held up a hand to halt Achara in mid-sentence.

"Let me explain," the princess said in hushed tones. "As a young boy he once saved my life. In eagle form—which you are now familiar with—I had been grounded by a hunter's arrow. Your grandfather found me in the forest, removed the arrow from my wing, and nursed me back to health.

"With the wing healed and set for me to fly away, I wanted to thank him for what he had done. When I spoke to him in human tongue and told him who I was and that he would someday have a granddaughter, someone that I had a future divine plan for, he was horror-struck."

"But...but... princess, why has Grandfather never mentioned you?"

"Oh, young lady—there is much you do not know. Your grandfather is a wise man and won't talk about it. I believe that to not be labelled a madman, he has tried to forget his encounter with a talking eagle."

"Divine plan? What divine..." In that instant, that precise moment, as Achara was about to ask what plan the princess had for her, the ground shook with such magnitude, with such immense force, she was knocked off her feet. Large rock slabs broke from the cave ceiling and splashed into the lake. As she tried to stand, a second blast threw her against the cave wall. Again, while on hands and knees, another shockwave tossed her into the churning water, its surface now roiling with fury. Terror shot through her like a flaming hot poker. Desperate, she looked to the princess for help.

"I...I...can't swim!" Achara wailed.

"The eagle, girl. Be the eagle. Quickly, take out the comb!" Princess Naw cried out.

Instantly, Achara was skimming in eagle form over the raging lake's water, the comb grasped tightly in her talons. Up the stone stairs and out of the narrow cave opening she flew with Shadow speedily running directly below her.

Tremors in Thandauan are so commonplace, seldom would a person even venture outdoors to question the danger.

Of two things, Achara was certain: first, an earthquake—a big one—was about to happen and second, she had to alert the sleeping townsfolk to awaken and flee the village. She feared the hodgepodge of small rocks, boulders, and trees now tumbling down the mountainside was only the beginning of something more disastrous than Thandauan had ever experienced.

With Shadow sprinting below, Achara raced down the mountainside. She beat her wings with all her might. Although the exhilaration of flying at such a speed was distracting, she couldn't help asking herself how Mother Nature could be so cruel. "Why? Why? Why?" she cried.

As another huge thunderclap resonated throughout the valley, large boulders, mud, and earth began to smash into the uppermost mountainside houses. Massive cracks appeared in the ground, swallowing up multitudes of trees and bushes. As the mountain shook with fury, farm animals dashed in panic down the buckling and twisting roads and pathways. Chaos ruled. Whole families huddled behind demolished houses and barns, while others ran in panicked circles. With the eagle's acute sense of smell she now possessed, the swirling dust mixed with the oppressive humidity clogged her nostrils, making flying difficult.

Achara flew through her grandfather's open bedroom window and landed heavily on his chest.

Hoping a talking eagle would not shock him this time, she screamed, "Grandfather, Grandfather. Wake up! Wake up! It's me, Achara. I need your help. Please...please...Get up! Get up, Grandfather! We must warn everyone the mountain is about to tumble down on the village. Go quickly. Ring the sunset bell with all your might. Take Shadow with you!"

Before she could utter another word, her grandfather was out the door, the tiger hot on his heels.

Achara fashioned a plan. As she swiftly flew back up the mountainside, she scanned the ground for any sign of the temple.

Her heart leapt with joy—badly damaged, but at least still standing, she whispered a thank-you to Mother Earth for sparing it from the already devastated landscape. She could also clearly hear the sunset bell over the din. *Thank you, Grandfather. Hopefully some will be saved.*

Doubtful a talking bird would be deemed credible by any of the villagers, she dropped the silver comb on the temple floor's centre, transformed back into human form, stepped out of the entry, and hollered for all to follow her inside.

Packed shoulder-to-shoulder, safely under the roof, she ordered all to tightly close their eyes and hold hands in a circle around the comb. As the walls of the temple began to collapse, a large section of the roof tore away causing many to cry out in fear. But with little else to do, collectively the group complied with Achara's commands. Without the help of lights, the entire spectacle was swathed in a depressing darkness.

Again in eagle form, she flew above their heads. Around and around the room—faster and faster she flew. But nothing seemed to be happening.

Please, please, Buddha...please...

Through the crescendo of crashing rocks, smashing glass, and ear-piercing wails from the panicked group, the despondency she felt only steeled her determination.

My plan has to work, or all is lost.

Faster and lower she flew, her wings a blur, her talons sometimes brushing the heads of the taller townsfolk.

No sooner than she had lamented, "Is my plan a foolish idea?", than another wave of massive rocks and debris crashed through the temple walls and passed *through* the entire group—still with eyes clenched and holding hands tightly to the next—as if they were never there.

Achara, now giddy with elation, cried out, "It worked, my crazy plan actually worked! Thank you, Princess Naw, thank you, Mother Nature, thank you, Mighty Buddha, thank you Grandfather, thank you…Thank you, everyone!"

The heavens opened to bright moonlight and shining stars. The depressing darkness that had enveloped the temple—or what was left of it—was now swathed in brightness.

But as rapid as the entire catastrophe had unfolded, a sludge-like stillness hung in the air—a deafening silence.

"Where is the circle? Where did they go?" Achara cried aloud. "Oh no! They're still invisible. Must the comb be removed for them to re-appear? But...but, I must find it. Where is it?" she bellowed.

Achara, again in human form, frantically began to claw through the rubble. Terror tore at her heart. With her flesh now torn from her hands, she cried out "Please ...please can somebody help me?"

Panic-stricken, she did not hear her grandfather and Shadow enter. Not having expected aid to arrive so quickly, she jumped at her Grandfather's answer.

"We're here, Achara. What is it you so desperately need help with?"

Achara began to cry. Tears flowed freely down her cheeks. "A comb, Grandfather. A silver comb. Oh please, please…"

"There, there, little bird. How can you see what you search for through eyes filled with tears?

We will find your precious comb. I have no doubt."

— — —

Nestled in a flowerbed in the town square on a stone pedestal a bronze statue of a young girl stands, an eagle perched on her shoulder and a tiger lying at her feet. There is no plaque, sign or nameplate commemorating its existence.

Seldom will first-time visitors get an explanation of its significance. It is part of a happy legend few locals will talk about—a legend of how a local girl, who long, long ago miraculously saved an entire village. Not one person or animal perished that day.

They prefer to have the tour companies take the curious up Naw Bu Baw's Mountain, as it is known locally, to a small blue sign mounted on a precariously positioned rock. They then recount the well-versed legend of how a princess's witchcraft trial once took place on that exact spot.

Mere Rain is an international nonentity of mystery whose library resides in California.

Mere likes travel, food, art, and of course, reading. Mere enjoys fairy tales, fantasy, mythology, and mysteries.

Mere Rain has published short stories with Mischief Corner Books, The Mad Scientist Journal, and Things in the Well.

A Gentler Blow

By Mere Rain

Eresh watched the landscape drawing closer beneath the plane. They had passed over sharp, brown-striped mountains shaped like the blade of an ax, and then over a tan plain crossed by a river with oddly pink banks. Eresh didn't know the names of the mountains or the plain or the river. The outline of the city of Shiraz was unfamiliar, and when they landed she wouldn't know the names of the streets or where anything was.

At home in Rochester she had been allowed to take the bus by herself since she had started middle school. She knew which historical figures the bridges were named after, and that older people called the Metropolitan the Chase Tower, and that Genesee meant *beautiful valley* in Iroquois. If she got lost here would she even be able to ask for directions?

The adults were murmuring to one another in Avestan, of which Eresh understood only a few dozen words. They did that sometimes, although they usually spoke English at home. All of them but Uncle Ardash had been born in America. It was weird to see her mom and aunts with their hair covered. It was like they were different people now that they were in another country.

As they exited the plane they switched to Persian, which Eresh knew a little better but still not very well. It didn't matter, her parents had assured her, because Yima and some other relatives were meeting them at the airport in Shiraz, and they spoke English.

Yima was an older cousin, practically grown up now, who had been studying in Iran for several months, living with distant relatives. His parents and hers, and some other aunts and uncles, had decided it was a perfect time to revisit the land of their ancestors.

Yima smiled when he saw them in the baggage claim. It made Eresh realize how rarely he smiled usually, although he was one of the kindest of her cousins, one who had never pushed or scolded her when she was small or said she couldn't do things because she was a girl. But he had always been serious and a little distant, and he seemed even more so now as he greeted his own parents formally in Avestan, bowing before kissing their cheeks. He too was a different person here, a grown-up in a dark coat and slacks instead of worn jeans and a U of R sweatshirt, speaking a language she couldn't understand.

Yima introduced the relatives with him, a muscular middle-aged man he called Uncle Aftab and Aftab's pretty, bright-eyed daughter, Mehrab. They weren't really her or Yima's uncle and cousin, but related in some more distant way she hadn't understood when her grandfather showed her his genealogical charts. But they smiled and nodded at all the American cousins, and Mehrab asked in English, with only a slight accent, if they'd had a good flight and if they needed anything before the drive. Eresh's mother and grandmother always asked people if they needed a snack.

Then they and their mountain of luggage were being loaded into three SUVs. Yima patted her head as he handed her into a waiting car. She would have objected to the childish gesture, but suddenly she could hardly keep her eyes open. What time was it here? She sagged against her mother's arm.

"Sleep, Eresh," her mother said. "It's a long drive."

She nodded. Her parents had told her they would be visiting their relatives near Shiraz first, then seeing the sights of Tehran before they returned to the States. She wanted to see

Shiraz and the countryside, but the car was stuffy with the heat on, and she was too sleepy. On the other side of their mother, her younger brother, Bardiya, was already slumped, mouth hanging open. Eresh settled herself more securely and let her eyes drift closed.

She half woke when her father carried her from the car, getting a vague impression of bushes and trees as she was carried inside and tucked into bed.

***

Eresh woke early in the morning to cool, clean air and the sound of birds calling. She thought she had been wakened by someone saying her name, but there was no one. The room was small and bare—not like her room at home, a mess of colorful toys and books and clothing—but there was nothing strange about it. Just a white-painted square with wooden floorboards, a woven rug, and a dresser. Her suitcase sat next to the chest of drawers.

Eresh needed the bathroom. She left the warmth of the blankets and poked her head out of the door. She could smell barbari bread baking, just like her grandmother made for breakfast at home. She found the necessary room just across the hall and used it. The oval soap had the same rose-and-spice scent as the handmade soaps her family used.

Uncertain where to go next, she tiptoed along the hall until she heard voices. They led her to the kitchen, where her parents were drinking tea while two women, one middle-aged and one old, prepared lavash.

"Ah, Eresh, come in," her father called.

"You slept good, malus?" her mother asked. "You weren't cold?"

"I was fine, mom."

"Eresh, this is Aftab's wife, Aunt Sanaz, and his mother, Mrs. Narges."

"Call me Auntie Jah," the old woman said in Persian.

Eresh's father glanced at her and opened his mouth.

"Hengam bekam, Auntie," Eresh said quickly, to show that she understood.

"Good, good." Auntie Jah smiled and nodded. "Have tea, dear." She poured a glass and set it down by the sugar bowl. "You're hungry?"

"Yes, please, Auntie." Smelling the fresh bread reminded Eresh that she had missed dinner. She put quince jam on the warm lavash and tried not to eat it too quickly.

Eresh had assumed that everyone else was still asleep, but while she was eating, Yima, Mehrab, Uncle Aftab and another, older man she hadn't met before came in, wearing heavy coats and looking sweaty and tired. The Aunties poured more tea.

"This is Uncle Omid," Eresh's father told her. Her parents must have stayed up and met everyone last night.

"What happened to your hand?" Eresh asked Yima, spotting scraped knuckles as he lifted his tea.

"I tripped. We were hiking."

"In the dark?"

"Getting in shape before pigging out on holiday food!" Mehrab put in with a laugh.

"No one here needs to lose weight," Aunt Sanaz said firmly, piling lavash on a platter. "Eat, eat," she directed. "You have more, little one. You're eleven? Still growing. Take some feta for strong bones."

Mehrab went to the fridge and produced a bowl of cucumber and tomato salad.

"I'm making egg and spinach kuku," Aunt Sanaz said. "It'll be ready in a minute."

"Great, mama. Is there coffee?" Mehrab poured for the four of them and started a new pot.

Soon, more unfamiliar people crowded into the kitchen, some in pajamas and others already dressed. Only Bardiya and Cousin Vahram were still asleep.

"Will you go fetch the boys, honey?" Eresh's mother asked her husband. "Eresh, help me carry the dishes to the dining room."

"I'll help," Mehrab said. "I don't cook, except salads and sweets."

"I'll bring the glasses." Yima managed to pick up three with each hand without spilling. Mehrab gave him a twinkling smile in thanks. Were they dating, Eresh wondered? It wasn't like they were very related, and Mehrab was awfully pretty, and she supposed Yima was good-looking, in a severe and sharp-featured way. If they got married, would he stay here in Iran? Or would she move to Rochester, like Uncle Ardash? How had Uncle Ardash and Auntie Shai met, anyway?

Her father came in with a bleary and befuddled Bardiya. There weren't two chairs together, so he tried to put Bardiya on his lap. Bardiya pulled away indignantly. He was eight but acted younger when he was tired.

"Here, Barda, have half my chair," Eresh said quickly, before he could make a fuss. Bardiya squeezed in next to her and leaned shyly against her while she put bread and jam on a plate for him.

A few minutes later Cousin Vahram came in with wet hair. He sat with his parents, further down the table, avoiding "the kids," as he had started calling them when he turned thirteen a few months ago. Uncle Ardash spoke in Persian to an old man, too quickly for Eresh to understand. Auntie Jah,

Auntie Shai and a woman in her thirties discussed what needed to be done for the impending winter solstice party.

"Of course everything has been cleaned," the woman said. "And the men have built the bonfire, and we've cooked a lot."

"There's still more to cook," Auntie Jah said. "I need some spices."

"Yes, and we'll want more rice and eggs," Sanaz put in as she delivered the kuku to the table.

"And almonds and barberries," Auntie Jah continued. "Mehrab, take them to the Vakil Bazaar. You can get the spices, and the children can buy some sweets and see the stalls. Show them the artisans and antique dealers."

"Yes, and take them to see some of the outdoor tourist attractions," Sanaz said. "It's not bad today, but it's forecast to get colder after Yalda. The solstice is when winter weather really sets in. It might rain next week. You should go see the sights now."

"All right. Better pack a week's worth of food, then," Mehrab said, laughing.

Her mother swatted her shoulder but immediately said. "Well, of course I'll make some snacks. You can't take visitors out without food."

"Oh, Mama. I was kidding. There's plenty of places to buy lunch. You have too much to do already."

"But those bought meals are never healthy," Sanaz fretted. "Buy some fruit and vegetables."

"I'll buy all the food in the city! Don't worry. Come on, cousins, get dressed and we'll beat the traffic."

Eresh left Vahram eating breakfast and led her brother to the bathroom for a quick wash. Then she laid out a warm outfit and left him to put on while she unpacked and changed into clean clothes. She collected Bardiya on the way back to the kitchen, where Aunties Sanaz and Jah were murmuring to each other as they packed snacks and double-checked their supply of staples.

After the third time Auntie Jah took back the list to make sure an item was on it, Mehrab said, "Just call me if you think of something more!" and led the way to the cars.

***

The streets were crowded with people out shopping, or driving to relatives' homes for the holiday. Eresh peered through the car window. She wasn't used to anyone other than her family celebrating Yalda, so she was eager to see what it was like here. Did they put up lights like most of her classmates did for Christmas? Did they celebrate Christmas at all?

Eresh had pictured a bazaar as an outdoor market, like movies set in the Middle East always showed, but it turned out to be a huge, old building. It was even more crowded inside than the street had been.

"Mehrab, show the children some of the interesting stalls while I buy spices," Sanaz ordered. "Don't lose them."

At first they just walked around, admiring the colour and bustle. Tall piles of carpets and heaps of bright spices and racks of shoes or pots and pans fought for space. The scents of cardamom and saffron, leather and wool, iron and rose water all mixed confusingly. Eresh almost walked into a baby carriage while craning her neck to admire the ceiling, which came to a point high above and was painted with decorative designs.

"I want to look at this shop," Bardiya announced, tugging Eresh to a halt.

"Jewelry is for girls, Barda," Vahram told him.

"Boys can wear it if they want," Eresh argued.

Bardiya ignored them both. "I want to buy something for Miss Ronny." Ms. Aronberg was his teacher.

"I'm going to watch that man making the rug," Vahram said. Both sets of parents followed him to watch the loom being operated.

Eresh quickly choose a copper bangle with pink glass beads as a souvenir for her best friend, Nola. Barda lingered indecisively, trying to find the very best bauble for the object of his affection. Eresh browsed idly. She thought someone called her name from behind her and turned but didn't see anyone she knew. As she looked back and forth, the packed shelves of the antique dealer in the next stall caught her eye. She sighed wistfully.

"Not interested in jewelry?" Mehrab asked. "Go to one of the nearby shops if you want. I'll watch him and come get you when he's done."

"You're sure you don't mind? Thanks! Barda, I'm just going to the next shop. You stay with Cousin Mehrab, okay?"

"Okay," Bardiya agreed absently, staring at rows of dangling earrings with enamel flowers in different colors and sizes.

The antique shop was fascinating just to wander around. Its shelves were cluttered with all sorts of things, some shiny and others dull and dirty. Eresh didn't know anything about antiques except from Indiana Jones movies. Some of the stuff looked like broken junk, while other objects were fancy enough for a museum.

There were shelves of metal teapots with floral patterns, and one with an elongated cat for a handle, which she quite liked. She turned over the grubby price tag and winced. Enameled boxes. Pots and vases with incised designs. Plates with pictures formed from variously coloured metals. Worn coins in individual plastic boxes, with labels she couldn't read. Lighter items of furniture, like wooden chairs and coffee tables with curved legs.

At home the shelves of books would have drawn her, but she knew she wasn't likely to find anything in English. She poked about in a cracked wooden crate labeled "400K or less." That was about ten dollars, wasn't it?

There was a lot of chipped pottery, marked down to a buck or two. Jewelry in plastic baggies, with stones missing. Dented metal bowls. Half a book; sad. As she was trying to push aside some stained weaving, her fingers brushed something with an odd set of pointed ridges. She felt along them and found a smoother part that fit into her palm like a handle. She pulled the thing free—it weighed several pounds, which was probably why it had slid to the bottom of the crate—and examined it.

The object was metal, about a foot long, and certainly looked old, but beyond that Eresh was mystified. There was the ridged end, which she had felt, then the smooth cylinder that did indeed seem to be a handle, then three curved prongs, sort of like a trident. It felt comfortable and balanced in her hand, but she couldn't imagine what it was for. If it really cost less than ten dollars, she would buy it and ask her relatives if they knew.

Eresh approached the man behind the counter. His wide back was to her, curved almost into a sphere over a book with crumbling pages. She couldn't see his face. "Bebakhshid," she ventured. *Excuse me.* "Farsim xub nist." *I don't speak Farsi very well.* "How much is this?"

Without looking up, he stretched out one very large, long-fingered hand and wrote on the receipt pad: 129,600. Only about three dollars. She even had exact change. She laid the money on the counter. The man still didn't look around.

Eresh thanked him. "Sepasgozaram." He didn't respond. She tucked her purchase into the book bag she had used as a

carry-on, carefully settling the heavy object at the bottom, under Nola's bracelet and the book she was supposed to read for English class. Then she left, oddly disappointed she hadn't seen the antique dealer's face or heard his voice.

Mehrab and Bardiya were at the weaver's stall with the rest of the group. The loom was pretty neat, although Eresh sure wouldn't have wanted to spend all day sitting at it. Mehrab was frowning at her phone.

"Is something wrong?" Eresh asked as she came to stand beside her cousin.

"Oh, here you are, Eresh." Mehrab smiled. "Nothing wrong, just reading the news. There's always bad news, you know." She shifted to texting. "The shopping is done, so as soon as—Hi, mom! Let me take that. No, give me the heavy one. I thought since it's nearby we'd go to the Pars Museum, even though it's kind of boring—" Mehrab was cut short by a generalized scolding about not valuing the heritage of Persia. She winked at Eresh. "So you all want to go, then? Come on."

The building was very beautiful, but Eresh privately agreed the museum was kind of boring. There was a lot of information she couldn't read. Vahram told her it was about the history of the city. She didn't pay much attention. She felt oddly tired even though it was the middle of the day. If she had been younger she would have been leaning on her mother the way Bardiya was doing. She stared dreamily at two tall stone carvings, a bearded man with wings and a man with the head of an eagle. They had their hands were raised the way the pastor at Nola's church did when he said blessings. Eresh's eyes drifted closed, and for a second the two blessing hands seemed to move.

"Wake up!" Vahram elbowed her.

"Maybe time for lunch," Sanaz suggested. "Come, we'll have a picnic. You must see the Qur'an Gate. It is a thousand years old!"

"It's in a park," Mehrab explained as they walked back to the cars. "And on the way there, I'll detour past the Pink Mosque. It's really pretty."

The mosque was pretty, although it didn't seem especially pink. Vahram pointed this out.

"It's the glass that's pink," Mehrab explained. "I guess it's really colorful when the sun shines through it."

"Wow!" Eresh exclaimed. "That's all glass?"

"Can we see it from inside?" Vahram asked.

"I don't know," Mehrab admitted. "I'm not sure if it's allowed for non-Muslims to go in." The adults glanced at one another, shrugging. Apparently none of them had visited a mosque. "I'll look it up later," Mehrab decided. "If it is permitted, we can take a tour of some of the older ones, too."

The Qur'an Gate was impressively large, big enough for cars to pass under, and offered a great view of the city. The adults all took pictures with their phones, then made the children stand together under the big arch. Then they ate lunch. In addition to the bread and salads and cold cuts Sanaz had packed, they had bought fruit and sweets at the Bazaar.

After the picnic they went home, because there were still more dishes to prepare for the holiday feast. Auntie Shai saw Bardiya yawning and said, "You kids take a nap, or you won't be able to stay up tonight."

"I'm too old for naps," Vahram beat Eresh to arguing.

His father raised an eyebrow. "Suit yourself, but don't complain if you're too tired to enjoy Yalda."

Suddenly, Eresh could barely keep her eyes open. She went to bed and drifted off to the distant, comforting murmur of the adults talking as they cooked.

***

Eresh was woken much later by red beams of evening sun crossing her face. She rubbed her eyes and went to lean out the window. She hadn't had a chance to look around the family residence yet, except to see that it was large and had a garden around it. She looked one way and saw the front gates and the residential street lined with other large houses, the direction they had gone before. When she turned the other way, she saw an even larger garden, with planted beds near the house, and then an orchard. Beyond that was barer ground with rocks and shrubs, leading to low hills. The house must be on the very edge of the city.

As Eresh stood gazing, lights began to come on in other homes, and she could smell the smoke of holiday fires. Time to celebrate the solstice. She ran to take a quick bath and change into a heavy red sweater and warm corduroy pants.

When she reached the kitchen, Auntie Jah slipped a red and gold ribbon over Eresh's head. On it was a nazar, a blue glass eye bead, to ward off evil.

"A good Yalda!" Auntie Jah said. "Carry this bowl for me, Eri-naz." She handed the girl a big trencher full of sliced watermelon. "It's not too heavy?"

"No, Auntie, I'm fine. Happy Yalda." The big dining room had been rearranged so the table stood against the wall as a buffet. She put the bowl down next to a pyramid of pomegranates and went out the open double doors to the garden. There was a paved area with an awning over it, then a wide, clear space where several Uncles were lighting the bonfire. It would be kept going all night to keep away demons and bad luck.

Old-fashioned music was playing on an old-fashioned record player, and an older aunt whose name she hadn't learned yet was singing along with it as she cracked almonds into a bowl. Suddenly Eresh was homesick for her grandparents, who played this sort of music at Yalda. She had never spent a holiday away from them before.

Yima and Mehrab talked with Yima's parents, all holding glasses of tea. Her parents sat on a bench, Barda between them, their arms around each other's shoulders. No one had noticed her lingering by the door.

Eresh went back to the kitchen to see if Auntie Jah needed more dishes carried in. The old woman smiled at her. "Kufteh?" She offered a meatball on a fork. It was similar to the ones they made at home, but a little sweeter, like it had some sort of fruit in it. Eresh made an appreciative noise and carried the dish to the next room. This time Jah followed behind her with a bowl of paneer in one hand and borani in the other.

Yalda wasn't like Christmas dinner, which she had gone to at Nola's house: people didn't sit down to eat a big meal, instead they nibbled all night. There was probably a rice casserole in the oven, and something stewing on the stovetop. Skewers of meat and vegetables were waiting to be cooked once the fire had settled to an even blaze.

Uncle Omid stood with a book open in his hands, and the family quieted to hear the first poem of Hafez. Eresh could only pick out words here and there, but he was a good reader, and she let the rhythm of the verse flow over her as she watched the flames leap higher and the stars appear one by one.

By midnight Eresh was full and getting sleepy. She got up and wandered around to stay awake. Mehrab stood near the fire, speaking with her own parents and Yima's. She looked serious and a little sad. Eresh wondered if she was sad because Yima wasn't with her. Eresh looked around for Yima, but couldn't see him. She walked around all the little clusters of relatives, then into the house and out again, more than enough times that if he had been in the bathroom he would have been done by then.

"Where's Yima?" she asked Auntie Shai.

"He had to go out—"

"On Yalda night! Isn't that bad luck?"

"He'll be back soon, dear. Now, go see if Auntie Jah needs any help, please."

Eresh glanced around periodically, but never saw her cousin. Some hours later, Uncle Ardash and Uncle Aftab disappeared as well -- but they came back a little while later and stood talking to Auntie Shai, who frowned. Eresh thought about getting up and going to hear what they were saying, but Bardiya was asleep against her shoulder, and she was comfortable and drowsy.

Eventually it was time for a last sweet, a last glass of tea, a final poem by the dying fire. Then the sun peeked through the trees and everyone clapped and went to bed.

***

When Eresh woke it was noon. They ate leftovers for lunch and took turns doing heaps of dishes. Yima wasn't among them, but no one remarked on his absence.

He was there for dinner, looking tired and a little pale.

"Are you okay, Yim?" Eresh asked.

"Just a little under the weather," he told her with a sad smile.

Before she could ask more, Auntie Jah leaned over him, depositing a bowl of thick green goop. "You eat ash," she ordered. "Good for you."

Spinach, yuck.

Planning to see more sights tomorrow, everyone went to bed early.

Eresh woke in the night. The house was quiet and dark, but thought just before she opened her eyes, she had heard a woman crying for help. She strained her ears but there was nothing. Not even the night birds, not even the breeze. How silent it was.

She didn't want to wake people for no reason. They were all tired after staying up the previous night. But what if she hadn't dreamed the sound, and someone was in trouble? She would go just as far as the back gate and see if she heard anything more.

Eresh got out of bed and slipped her bare feet into her boots, then pulled her jacket on. It hung more heavily to one side. She put her hand in the pocket and found the strange metal object she had gotten at the market. When had she put that in her coat pocket? She was surprised it fit. It felt good in her hand, though, and it was heavy enough to hit someone with. Clutching it for security, she crept along the hall to the back door.

The garden was silent too, not a leaf rustling. She followed the path to the gate, her footsteps silent as well. She tried to peer through the bars of the gate, but it was dark, only a few dim solar lights illuminating nothing but shrubbery. The front of the house, facing the street, had streetlamps and a sidewalk, but the back garden let out onto uneven, open fields and low, stony hillocks. Who would be out there at night?

Eresh was just turning to go back to the house when she heard the cry again. Spinning back to the dark, she brushed against the gate, and it eased open a fraction. Before she had time to think about it, she had stepped over the threshold into the open night.

Once she had moved away from the blur of the artificial lights, the starlight was bright enough for her to make her way across the irregular ground without tripping. She wondered nervously if there were dangerous animals, or poisonous snakes. Once she jumped at a hissing noise, like a snake, but it wasn't nearby and she told herself it was a breeze rustling the grass. Then she heard a thin shriek and a thud. Eresh gasped and clutched her weapon to her chest. Heart pounding, she forced herself to keep walking.

She thought about someone out here alone, maybe hurt. They must be so scared. More scared than Eresh was. She made herself move faster.

Eresh rounded a boulder and froze. Only yards away, down a slight slope, Yima was struggling with a woman whose mouth was open impossibly wide around dark, crooked teeth. She had long nails and was trying to claw his face, but he held her wrists and dodged her kicks. When Eresh had gotten over the immediate shock of the sight, she looked past them and saw something even more frightening: a man lay on the ground, clutching at a sword that pierced his chest.

Yima let out a yip of pain as the woman's foot struck his shin. Eresh saw the fabric of his jeans darken with blood. She stared at the woman's feet. They were bare—and clawed! Eresh leapt forward and swung the metal object at the woman's head. It was heavy enough that it should have been a painful blow, but as it touched the woman's temple, it paused gently, as if something invisible cushioned it.

The woman collapsed.

Yima staggered back, catching Eresh's arm and drawing her away from the fallen woman. Keeping Eresh behind him, he pulled the sword out of the man—or was he a man? He was even more deformed than the woman, his skin gray and coarse and his mouth full of too many protruding fangs. The hands that had gripped the blade in his chest were clawed. Yima put the point of the sword in the fallen man's neck and leaned on it, severing his head. Eresh recoiled, but the fallen man didn't move. No blood came from the gaping wound.

Yima staggered back to the woman, bending to take her pulse and peer into her eyes. Then he returned to Eresh and hugged her with his free arm. She was trembling.

"Are you all right?" he asked. "What are you doing out here?"

"I heard her—" Eresh stopped. She couldn't have heard this fight from inside her room, no matter how loudly the woman had screamed. "Something woke me, and I thought I heard someone call for help. So I went outside, and then I heard... But..." She looked at her cousin.

"You hit her with this?" Yima carefully touched a finger to the blunt end of Eresh's weapon. "Where did you get it?"

"I bought it at the bazaar. Do you know what it is?"

"I've only seen pictures, but I think it must be Sharur, the mace of the god Ninurta. Our family has a story that Ninurta gave Sharur to a mortal to help her fight demons."

"Demons..."

"Yes. There are many kinds, with different names. The dew, the daeva." Yima pointed at the decapitated man. "That one there was a mainyu, an evil spirit wearing a corpse. They have to eat people to keep the corpse from rotting. I didn't kill that man; he was already dead. I just drove the demon out. The woman was human, but on her way to becoming a demon. There are other sorts. And as you saw, their bodies can be defeated by ordinary weapons—my sword is a just a sword—but the demons aren't destroyed. They escape back to wherever they come from. Sharur can truly end them. And more importantly, Sharur can heal those who have been influenced by the demons."

"Heal?"

"Yes, look." He drew Eresh closer to the fallen woman, patting her shoulder reassuringly when she hesitated. The woman hadn't moved, but her teeth and feet looked normal now. Her face was pale and lined, like someone who had been sick.

"I think what you heard earlier was Sharur guiding you to this spot. Legends say he speaks to the one who holds him, advising them. Thousands of years ago, they said he brought messages from the god Ninurta."

"Do you believe that?"

Yima looked into the distance. "Gods? I don't know. I've seen a lot of strange things. A lot of frightening things. If there are evil powers, I think there must be good ones as well. At least, I hope so."

"So... Do I give this to you?" Eresh held out Sharur. It was surprisingly difficult to uncurl her fingers from the handle. The mace, which looked so uneven, balanced perfectly on her palm.

He shook his head. "If it were for me, I would have found it myself. I already have my job, hunting evil. The healing is for you, if you're willing."

He paused, and Eresh shivered, thinking about facing more fanged, clawed things. Maybe by herself next time, without Yima around to be the grown-up.

"But listen, Eri," he went on. "Being a hero isn't only risking your life to fight monsters in the night, and sometimes being hurt. It's also missing parties, and being alone on holidays, and lying to your friends, and not having a normal life with a family."

That sounded pretty hard. Harder than braving the night and hitting the screaming lady had been. But she didn't feel like she could say, "No, I don't want to," when people who didn't have Sharur were getting eaten by monsters. She thought about how tired Yima looked some days.

"You were doing this at home, too, weren't you? Going out at night to fight the demons."

"That's right. Since I was about your age."

"Your mom and dad know, don't they? That's why they didn't search for you on Yalda, even though your mom looked worried."

"That's right. All our relatives here know, too. That's why I came. Uncle Omid was a demon hunter when he was younger. He's teaching me more about them, so I can learn to find them before they hurt people. Because, see, one of the things about demons is that they go after people who are good, or kind, or generous, because the demons want the world to be a worse place."

Eresh swallowed. "I was really scared," she whispered. "When you were my age, were you scared?"

Yima sighed. "I'm still scared, Eri."

Eresh looked down. Her hands were still clasped around Sharur's handle. She was already so used to holding it that she had forgotten. She was still scared, but she was angry, too—angry at the demons for being horrible and selfish and unfair, angry at them for hurting innocent people, and for making Yima have to be a hero instead of a regular kid and miss parties and fight and get hurt. Probably soon she would get hurt, too.

She squeezed Sharur with one hand and Yima's hand with the other and said, "I'll help."

Jessica Renwick is the author of the Starfell series for middle grade children. The first book in the series, *The Book of Chaos*, has won several awards including the Children's Literary Classics Gold award for Middle Grade General. She loves visiting schools and meeting readers at various book signings and events across Alberta. In addition to reading and writing, she enjoys a hot cup of tea, gardening, and outdoor adventures. Jessica lives in Red Deer, Alberta with her partner and pets. You can find her online on Facebook, Instagram, and at https://www.jessicarenwickauthor.com.

The Witch's Staff

By Jessica Renwick

Heather ran down the worn path through the forest. She glanced over her shoulder, wishing she were at home, curled up on her family's couch with a book and a bowl of strawberry ice cream. That had been her after-school plan, before she made the mistake of taking this shortcut through Wildwood Park. Now, she was fleeing from the biggest bully at Leafside Middle School. And he was gaining on her.

Carter Morgan was the meanest kid in Heather's grade. And to make things worse, he was also the most athletic. The star of the town's peewee hockey team, he was everything that Heather wasn't—confident, popular, and a very fast runner.

Heather's toe caught on a tree root, and she skidded to her knees. She scrambled to get up, but it was too late. Carter stood over her, a vicious smirk on his face.

"Give it here, horse face."

"Give what here?" Despite Heather's effort to sound fierce, her voice shook. She wiped her now dirty hands on her jeans and attempted to rise.

Carter pushed her back down to the ground. She landed on something hard and bumpy, and bit back a yelp.

"I told you, give it here. I know you stole Ashley's iPod." Carter loomed over her, sneering.

"I did not!" Heather blinked back tears. "My parents got that for me for my birthday. Mom even labeled it with my name." She pulled the pink iPod from her pocket and showed him the label: Heather Starling. There was a doodle of a daisy next to her name.

"Says you." Carter snorted and snatched the iPod from her hand.

She swallowed a sob.

Carter turned the device in his hands, inspecting the label. "I bet you put your name on it after you took it. Ashley told me she saw you steal it from her backpack. You think I'd believe *you* over *her*?"

Heather bit her lip, and a tear slid down her cheek. "Give it back."

"Oh, now you're going to cry like a baby?" he asked with a cocky grin.

Heather wished she could wipe that smile off his stupid face. Instead, she rubbed away the tear and shifted uncomfortably. She was sitting on a knobby root and oddly, it was warm. Much warmer than the mossy earth around it and growing hotter.

Carter pocketed the iPod and shook his fist at her. "I'll give you something to cry about."

The root flared with heat. Heather let out a squeak and rolled sideways off it. She righted herself and glanced over her shoulder, and her eyes widened. It wasn't a root at all. It was a walking stick, covered with a twisted carving of vines and leaves. The handle was sculpted into the roaring head of a bear—and that bear was glowing brightly.

Heather's jaw dropped.

Carter bent over with laughter. "Look at you, rolling around like a pig in the mud!" In his amusement, he hadn't noticed the bear staff yet.

A tingle of warmth spread through Heather's veins, and she grabbed the staff with both hands. She had no idea what compelled her, but she pointed it at him.

"Give it back."

He stopped laughing and stared at the cane. "What is that?"

Heather got to her feet, now holding the staff in two hands, still pointed at the boy. "It's a magic wand— er—cane."

Carter shot her a mirthless smile. "Are you serious, horse face? Do you really think that's magic?"

Heather took a shaking step back, wielding the staff like a two-handed sword.

Carter stomped over to her and grabbed its end. As he tried to wrench it from her grasp, Heather felt a bolt of heat sear through her. There was a flash of bright green light, and she was suddenly surrounded by acrid smoke.

Carter released his grip on the staff.

"What on earth was that?" She coughed and waved a hand in front of her face, clinging to the cane with the other. She rested the bottom on the ground and grasped the head of the bear, gazing at it with wonder. The wood had cooled beneath her fingers, and the glow was gone.

A gruff voice sounded through the smoke. "Oh, crap. You've gone and set it off! How'd you do that?"

Heather peered around but couldn't see anybody through the thick haze. Not even her attacker. "Who...who's there? Carter?"

"Never you mind, just lay down the staff and be on your way. The boy's gone."

A small breeze picked up and the smoke began to clear. Heather squinted through it, her pulse racing, and the outlines of a squat person and something round and scruffy appeared before her. The smoke thinned and the forms became clearer. A baby bear, wide-eyed and frightened, stared up at her. Beside it stood a man the size of a kindergartner with two short horns curving over his tousled auburn hair.

Heather squinted and shook her head. She had to be seeing things. From the waist down the man appeared to be a goat, with glossy brown hair that covered him from his ankles to his navel, two cloven hooves, and a short, twitching tail. The only clothing he wore was a burgundy vest with shiny gold stitching.

Her chest tightened and she stepped back, clutching the staff. "What are you? And where's Carter? Where did this bear come from?"

The man rubbed his temple, then held his hands out toward her. "Give me the staff."

Heather swallowed and pointed the stick at him. "Tell me who you are. And what happened to Carter."

The bear cub cowered and the peculiar man held up his hands. He took a step back. "Easy now. You obviously don't know what that thing can do in the right hands." He cast her a curious glance. "Why are you in the mortal realm, witch?"

"Witch? I'm not a witch." Heather wrinkled her nose. *What is he talking about?*

"You must have some sort of power."

Heather's heart beat wildly. What was going on here? Who was this...this creature? And why did he want this cane?

She put on what she thought was a brave face and cocked an eyebrow. She wiggled the wooden stick. "Tell me who you are. I'll use the wand if I have to."

The strange man looked her up and down, his brow furrowed, and he sighed. "It's a staff. And fine. But put that thing down. You're going to turn us all into squealing piglets." He gave her a sideways glance. "Or worse."

Turn us into piglets? The blood drained from Heather's face. She stood the staff on the ground—it was nearly as tall as her chin—and gripped it with white-knuckled fingers.

"My name is Basil, and this," the goat-man patted the trembling bear's head, "is your friend—or enemy, as it seems. Carter, is it?"

"What?" Heather's hands shook so hard she almost dropped the staff. "What do you mean, this," she jerked her head at the bear, "is Carter?"

Basil barked a laugh and shook his head. "Silly girl, that's what the staff does. You really aren't a witch then, are you?" He gave her a wary look. "That wand, as you call it, will turn us into forest creatures if you set it off again. Hand it over, for both our sakes."

Carter, the little bear, stared at Heather with wide amber eyes and let out a whine.

"No." She clutched the staff close to her chest. Her gaze slid from the carved bear handle to Carter then back again. *How is this possible*? She peered at the human footprints on the ground. The imprints of the boy's sneakers stopped right where the bear sat.

She bent down in front of the cub and placed her free hand on its head. "Carter?"

The bear lunged forward, barreling into her chest and knocking her off her feet. Heather hit the ground hard, the air forced from her lungs. She rolled onto her side and hugged the staff tightly, wheezing.

The cub snorted and glared down at her.

A howl of laughter met Heather's ears. Basil clapped his hands, a look of glee on his face. "See? It's the boy all right." He narrowed his eyes at the bear. "I can't say he doesn't deserve his fate, though."

The bear huffed and swung his thick head in Basil's direction.

"Oh, knock it off, you furry little beast," the goat-man said in a sharp voice. "I've dealt with a lot worse than you. I'm not afraid of a teddy bear."

Heather groaned and sat up, then scowled at the furry creature. "Okay. You're Carter, I get it."

The cub stomped the ground with his front paw.

Heather stared at the roaring head of the staff. If this cane had turned the boy into a bear, then it must have the power to turn him human again. She glanced at Carter, who glowered down at her with an open mouth and sharp, jagged teeth. An idea crept into her mind.

Heather stood and brushed the dirt from the back of her jeans with her free hand. Pushing down the panic in her chest, she set her jaw and stared defiantly at Basil. "I'm not giving you the staff." She turned to Carter. "If you ever want to be human again, you will stop bullying me."

Carter huffed and held up his paw as if to swing at her. Heather pointed the staff at him and summoned all the courage she had. "Next time, it'll be a mouse."

Basil chuckled and rubbed his rounded belly. "I wouldn't test her, bear."

The bear cub stared at her for a moment, then returned his paw to forest floor.

"Where's my iPod?" Heather asked.

The goat-man scratched his head. "Your what?"

"My—" She glanced around, looking for the pink device. "It's a pink box. Carter had it in his pocket."

"Ah." Basil tugged on his pointy beard. "Well, then it's wherever his clothes went. I'm not sure where the spell takes them."

Heather groaned. "The spell?"

Basil pointed at the bear. "What you did to him."

Carter sat down on his haunches and gave her a sour, strangely human look.

Despite what a jerk he was, she couldn't leave him like that. What would his parents do when a bear showed up at their front door? Nobody would believe her. He'd be shooed off to the forest to live his life as a grizzly.

Heather turned the staff in her fingers, thinking. After a moment, she spoke. "Stop being mean to me, Carter. You don't have to be nice, just civil. Heck, ignore me. But stop being so cruel."

The bear gazed at her intently, then gave her a slight nod.

Heather took that as an agreement. She glanced at the goat-man and wiggled the staff. "How do I turn him back?"

"You can't fix him with that." Basil rubbed his chin, looking at the plucky girl with renewed interest. "Circe uses a potion. But we can get one. I might be willing to help you."

Circe? She'd never heard of anybody with that name before. Could she trust the little demon—or whatever he was? Heather glanced at Carter, who had rolled onto his back and was playing with his baby bear paws. She sighed. What other choice did she have?

"What do I need to do?"

"I'll cut you a deal," Basil said with a gleam in his eye. "That staff—I need it gone. It's Circe's weapon, and she's after me. I'll help you get a potion if you give it to me."

"Circe?" Heather asked.

Basil let out a breath. "You know, the sorceress. Daughter of Helios and Perse."

Heather stared at him blankly.

"Right. I forgot. I'm in the mortal realm." He ran a hand through his tousled hair, avoiding the horns. "Circe is a powerful sorceress who turns people into animals using that staff." He pointed at the stick. "Her estate is full of woodland servants who were once men, and only she can break the spell with her potions. She's powerful, she's evil, and she's after me."

"Why?" Heather narrowed her eyes at him. "What did you do to her? And aren't you already, well, you know"—she swallowed—"some sort of animal?"

Basil scowled and stomped a hoof on the ground. "I'm a faun. And fauns are people, just like you. And I stole some apples from her orchard."

"That's it? She wants to turn you into a bear over some apples?"

Basil gave her a grim smile. "I'm sure she'll choose something more like a shrew. Or a slug." He grimaced. "And they aren't just apples. They're magic apples that give you youth and life. How do you think she's been around for thousands of years?"

Thousands of years? Heather's brows knit together. "What do you need them for? You seem young enough."

"It doesn't matter," Basil shot back. "I needed them, so I took them. But Circe found out, and now she's furious. She sent her wolves after me. So naturally, I outsmarted them and sneaked back to her palace. I stole the staff while she slept. Now she can't turn anyone into anything."

"Why didn't you use the staff to turn her into a rabbit or something?" Heather asked.

Basil tugged at his beard and gave her a sideways glance. "Because only a witch can make it wield magic. And she's the only one. That is, until you. Which is very strange, for a mortal. Very strange indeed."

"I'm no sorceress. I'm just a normal girl."

"Well, you're something. You're the only other person who's ever made the staff work."

Heather tapped her chin, thinking it over. *It has to be a fluke.* "So, if I give you the staff, you'll bring me a potion for Carter?"

"I'll bring you to Circe's palace, and you can get one yourself," Basil replied.

Heather had no idea who this Circe was or if she'd be willing to give away her magic. "You have to help me get the potion. I'm not giving you the staff until you do."

Basil crossed his arms and regarded Heather with a discerning gaze.

She twirled the staff in her fingers. "You never know, maybe I can turn him back into a human with this. Just because this Circe person can't doesn't mean that I can't."

Carter the Bear snorted and shuffled away from her.

The goat-man sighed and ran his hand over his face. "Stop, before you turn us all into pigeons. I'll take your deal. Follow me."

He turned and started down a lightly travelled game trail that forked off the main path. Heather followed, and the bear cub lumbered along behind her.

"Where are we going?" she asked.

"Circe's island," Basil replied over his shoulder.

Heather frowned. "How? We're in Alberta. We're not even close to the ocean."

Basil let out an amused snort. "You ask too many questions, young witch."

"I'm not a witch."

They plunged deeper into the forest. After about ten minutes the canopy of trees grew thicker, and the world beneath it darkened. Here, the mushrooms grew bigger. Lichen coated the trees. The air was fresh with the smell of pine and earth. Heather had never been down this little-used path before. The only other tracks on it were from wildlife. She glanced at Basil's cloven hooves. *Or maybe fauns.*

A few minutes later, they came to a stone wall draped with rope-like green vines. Basil stopped in front of it and pulled the vines to the side, like a curtain. Behind them was a battered wooden door. It looked ancient, with green moss growing up its side over a clunky metal latch.

"That's it?" Heather asked. "That's the door to your realm?"

"What were you expecting? Pearly gates?" Basil twisted the latch and pushed the door open. A burst of shimmery sunshine poured through the doorway into the dim forest.

Heather's heart skipped a beat. *It's real!*

Basil jerked his head. "Let's go, witch." He eyed the bear who stood beside her, gaping at the door. "Better leave him. Circe will want him for her collection." With that, he stepped through the doorway.

Heather turned to Carter. "I'm sorry, but you've got to stay. We can't have Circe kidnapping you."

Carter huffed and looked at her from the corner of his eye.

"I think it's best. Stay right here. We'll be back with the potion." She went to rub his ears, but he swatted her arm away with his paw.

"Sorry." She cringed. "For a second, I forgot you aren't a real bear. I'll try to be quick."

Basil's voice shouted at her through the door. "Are you coming, witch? Or have you decided to leave your friend as a bear?"

"Coming!" With one last glance at Carter, she took a deep breath, clutched the staff close to her, and stepped through the door into the bright sunshine on the other side.

The trees on this side were not the dense pines of Heather's home. These were ancient oaks with thick green leaves and gnarled trunks. The far-off sounds of waves and gulls met her ears. A warm breeze swept her hair from her face. She gazed at the door they had just come through. It looked the same on this side, worn yet solid. But instead of a stone wall, it was set into a tree trunk as wide as a car.

Basil was leaning up against a nearby tree with his arms crossed, waiting.

"Where are we?" Heather asked.

"Aeaea. Circe's island." He straightened, beckoned for her to follow, and took off down the path.

Heather walked behind him, holding the staff firmly and thumping it on the ground in time with her steps. It felt good in her hands—smooth, warm, and solid.

Basil slowed and let her catch up so they were walking side-by-side along the wide trail. "All right, witch, here's the plan. We have to sneak into Circe's kitchen. She stores her potions and herbs in the big pantry. We need the one with a blue glow. It'll be in a glass bottle with a cork stopper."

Heather nodded. "Glass bottle. Blue glow. Got it." *Should be simple, right*?

After a few minutes, the forest opened up to a grassy plain. A Grecian palace made from gleaming white stone with massive pillars stood on a cliff overlooking a sparkling blue sea. The air smelled of salt and sand. Heather resisted the urge to run to the beach. She'd never seen the ocean before.

She took a step forward, but Basil grabbed the back of her shirt and pulled her with him behind a tree. He held his fingers to his lips, peeked around the trunk, and pointed.

Heather followed his gaze, and her blood ran cold. At least a dozen predators were stalking through the long grass—mostly wolves, but she spotted a giant boar and a pair of hyenas. A full-sized brown bear lumbered near the treeline.

"What are they doing?" she whispered.

Basil pressed his lips together and frowned. "Guarding Circe. They were all people, once."

Heather swallowed. "How are we going to get by them?"

"Leave that to me." Basil winked, then pulled a flute from the inside pocket of his vest and began to play.

A sleepy melody floated through the air, and Heather's eyes began to droop. Basil stepped on her foot, jerking her awake, and kept playing. Soon, the predators on patrol laid down in the grass and closed their eyes. Even the bear, after one last yawn, hit the ground with a thud. His snores mingled with the flute's soothing song.

Satisfied his work was done, Basil pocketed the instrument. He gave a little bow and gestured towards the palace. "Shall we, witch?"

Heather clutched the staff to her chest and gingerly followed him through the tall grass. They crept by a snoozing hyena. Her heart raced when its lips twitched, revealing sharp fangs. But it let out a raspy breath instead of a growl and remained asleep.

Soon they were sneaking along the stone palace wall. Heather crouched low and did her best to keep up with the faun's quick pace. They slipped around the corner and stopped beneath an open window. Basil stood as tall as he could and peered through it.

"Kitchen's empty, and the pantry is wide open." He scrambled through the window and dropped softly to the floor inside.

Heather clambered after him but wasn't nearly as graceful. She dropped the staff, and it clattered on the marble floor.

Basil whirled toward her with a panicked look. He held his hands out in front of him and mouthed, *Don't move!*

Heather held her breath, but the kitchen remained quiet. It seemed nobody had heard her. She pulled the staff back to her side and gave Basil an apologetic smile.

Basil pointed at the pantry. They crept inside, and he closed the door gently behind them. There was a butcher block in the middle of the room, and on it rested an oil lamp and a heavy rounded pot. Heather swallowed. *A cauldron.*

Basil snapped his fingers and the lamp lit, casting a dim glow over the room. The two walls on either side were lined with drawers. Wooden barrels and boxes sat along the back wall. Various dried herbs hung from the ceiling, filling the room with the pungent smell of parsley and oregano.

"You have magic," Heather whispered. "Your flute, and the lamp . . ."

Basil shrugged. "Faun magic is simple. We can't make a stick turn people into beasts, or back into humans either." He gazed around the room. "Let's find that potion." He began to rummage through the shelf beneath the butcher block.

Heather leaned the staff against the counter beside her, opened the bottom drawer and began to search. It contained baskets of dried fruit. She moved to the next one and found glass jars filled with lentils. Definitely not what she was looking for.

"Her potion supplies are over here," Basil whispered as he dug into a drawer at the back of the room. "Dried herbs, feathers—" He pulled a jar into the light to inspect it. It was filled with a swampy green liquid and something lumpy floated in it. He frowned. "And whatever this is."

Heather shuddered, then stepped beside him. Basil pulled back an empty burlap bag to reveal a dozen tiny potion bottles stacked in a basket. One was giving off a dim blue glow.

A wide grin spread across his face. "Jackpot."

Padded footsteps sounded from the kitchen. Basil froze and cocked his ear to the door. Heather held her breath, afraid to move.

The footsteps stopped. A raspy, muffled voice floated through the door. "Do you think they've found the faun yet?"

"I doubt it, or they'd be back by now," a softer voice replied. "I'd hate to be here when they return with him."

"I wonder what she'll turn him into," the gravelly voice said.

"I don't want to know. He better get rid of the staff before they find him." The silky voice paused. "I hope he gets those apples to his brother in time. It's such a shame, that sickness she put on the boy. If Basil doesn't get him off this island to Asclepius soon, he's going to die."

Basil's brother? Heather's mind raced. *That's why he wanted the apples!* She glanced at the faun. He stared straight ahead, ignoring her gaze.

The deeper voice snorted. "It's his own fault, sneaking around her gardens. Why would anybody come near this place?" He paused. "Do you see her olives in the cupboard there, or do we need more from the pantry?"

The handle turned and Heather shrank even lower to the floor. Basil's face paled and he pulled the flute from his pocket.

"They're right here. Hurry up, we don't want to set her off again."

The handle popped back into place.

"What's she going to do? Turn me into a toad? Oh wait, she can't." Both voices snickered and then faded away.

Basil frowned. "That was close. Too close." He snatched the healing potion and handed it to Heather. "It's the only one. Keep it safe."

He grabbed the basket, emptied it into the drawer, then slung its handle over the crook of his arm. He walked to the back wall and pushed a wooden crate in front of one of the barrels.

Heather eyed the tiny glass bottle in her hand. "It's only got enough for one swallow."

"That's enough to fix him." Basil stepped onto the crate and peered into the barrel. "Now grab the staff. I'll just get a few more apples before I go."

Heather picked up the magical weapon. "Do you need help?"

Basil leaned over the lip of the barrel. "Just go! I'll meet you outside the window in a minute."

Heather shrugged and opened the door a crack to make sure the kitchen was empty. It was. She slipped from the pantry and moved stealthily to the window.

Just as her feet met the soft grass outside, there was a crash and the sound of apples tumbling over the floor. Heather's breath hitched. She peered back inside, but it was too late. With a thumping of monstrous feet, a huge gorilla rushed into the kitchen and yanked open the pantry door.

"Basil!" The gorilla had a familiar raspy voice. "Don't even think about playing that flute."

Heather waited below the windowsill, her heart racing, as the gorilla dragged Basil from the kitchen. She leaned on the staff and fingered the potion in her pocket, thinking. She could just leave. She had what she needed to turn Carter human again.

But what about Basil? Her heart twinged. *And his brother.*

The servant's words popped into her mind. *If Basil doesn't get the boy off this island, he's going to die.* She groaned. She couldn't leave her new friend.

Heather edged around the stone side of the palace, wondering where the gorilla was taking the faun. After turning another corner, she found herself facing a lush garden. Among the hedges and fruit trees, a beautiful woman lounged on a wicker chair. She wore a long white dress and had a crown made of antlers perched atop her flowing blonde hair. A bottle of wine sat on a table beside her, and a lion lay at her feet. He yawned and rested his shaggy head on the ground. A dozen other beasts paced around the perimeter of the garden, ready to pounce on anybody who dared approach.

Circe. Heather ducked behind a hedge, her heart hammering in her chest.

The gorilla burst from the palace door, carrying the squirming faun under one arm. Heather winced. *Poor Basil.* How was she going to save him with all these brutes around?

"What have we here?" Circe stood from her chair, her hands on her hips and a cruel smile on her face.

The giant ape dropped Basil on the ground at her feet. He landed on his bottom with an *oomph* and glared at the servant.

Circe narrowed her eyes. "Basil, you came back."

Basil got to his cloven feet and grunted. "I assure you, it wasn't to see your smiling face."

"I caught him stealing apples in the kitchen, my lady," the gorilla said.

Circe smirked, then waved her hand in the air. Ropes snapped into existence and wrapped around Basil's wrists and ankles. He fell to the ground with a thud.

She squatted next to him and ran a finger over his cheek. "What am I to do with you, faun? This is the second time you've been caught stealing from me."

Basil craned his head away from her. "If you'd lift your curse from my brother, I wouldn't need your darn apples."

Circe's face reddened, her beautiful features twisting into a scowl. "Your brother kidnapped my best fox and brought her to the earthly realm—"

"He didn't kidnap—"

"Enough!" Circe spat the word. She stood and her eyes darkened with fury. She jabbed Basil with a sandaled foot. "Alex is a traitor and deserves what he got. And you, daring to steal from your queen, are about to get what you deserve too."

Basil stiffened. "You're not my queen."

Circe bent down so her face was close to his. "Considering my staff has mysteriously disappeared, I suppose the only punishment I have for you is death."

Death? Heather's heart slammed against her ribs. *Think, Heather. You have to do something*!

Basil's face paled. "Do you really—"

Circe snapped her fingers and a gag appeared in Basil's mouth.

The servants began to howl and chatter. They paced back and forth, restless and agitated as if they were caged.

"Silence!" Circe cast a glare over the quivering beasts. They quieted, staring at her fearfully.

Heather closed her eyes and ran her hand over the head of the cane. It grew warm beneath her fingers. She knew what she had to do.

She took a deep breath and stepped out of hiding with the staff raised in front of her. "Stop! I have your staff. Let Basil go and I'll give it back."

Every face in the garden turned to Heather.

Circe cocked her head, peering at the girl. "Come here, child."

Heather tentatively walked through the garden past the gaping animals and stood in front of Circe. She lifted her chin to look the sorceress in the face, gripping the staff closely to her chest. "I believe you're looking for this. I'm willing to give it to you if you let Basil go."

Circe gave her an amused smile. "Where did you get this, mortal?"

Heather swallowed. "I found it."

Circe snarled and grabbed the staff with both hands. "How dare you, you little brat! This is rightfully mine."

She twisted, trying to wrench the staff free, but Heather dug her heels into the earth and held on.

The staff began to vibrate.

Circe yanked on it again, pulling Heather towards her. Despite her aching fingers, the girl hung on for dear life.

"You little fool!" Circe clenched her teeth and scowled. "If you don't let go, you'll be joining my servants as a dirty little muskrat!"

She jerked the staff straight up and Heather lost grip with one hand. She clung on to the cane with the other, now high above her head.

The animal servants began to cry out. Heather glanced at them. They howled frantically, but they weren't bristling or snarling. None of them tried to help their mistress.

The lion gave Heather a slight nod. He winked.

Circe's voice drew Heather's attention back to her. "What are you going to do, weak little mortal?" Her lips curled into a vicious grimace. "You dare think you're a threat to me? You're nothing!"

Circe yanked on the staff again. Heather hesitated and almost lost her grip on it.

Basil, who had worked the gag down over his chin, cried out, "You can do this, Heather! Look at what you did to Carter. Circe is just another big bully. I believe in you!"

Heather's resolve hardened. There was no way she could let Circe win. Not after seeing the devastation she had caused—the poor souls trapped here, the curse on Alex, the threat to murder Basil. Heather's cheeks grew hot, and the roaring bear on the staff began to glow.

Circe's eyes lit up and she let out a high-pitched cackle.

Heather lunged towards the witch, sending them both sprawling to the ground. She grabbed the staff with both hands and wrenched it from Circe's grasp. Heat seared through Heather's chest, and the entire garden was engulfed in thick black smoke.

Breathing heavily, Heather looked around. The staff lay next to her, no longer glowing, and Circe was nowhere to be seen. The garden was silent.

"H-hello? Basil?"

The faun stepped through the thinning smoke, free of his bonds. His eyes were wide as he helped Heather to her feet.

"Did she... did you?" His hands shook as he picked up the staff and handed it to her. He gazed at her with admiration and patted her on the back. "I knew you could do it."

Murmured voices broke through the haze. A joyous shout rang out.

Heather turned to the servants and her heart leapt. Men and women stood crowded in the garden, laughing and hugging each other. There were no animals in sight.

"We're free!"

"The girl turned us back!"

"Thank you, dear child!"

Heather gave Basil a bewildered look. "What happened?"

A white rabbit leapt from the tall grass where Circe had lain just moments before. With a strangled cry, it darted toward the forest.

Basil stroked his beard as it bounded away. "That'd be Circe. When you changed her, her magic must have broken. Too bad you didn't turn her into a snail. Or a centipede." He wiggled his eyebrows.

Heather swallowed. *I did that*? Did this mean Carter was human again, like Circe's servants?

"I have to go home." She checked her pocket; the tiny bottle was still intact. "If Carter is still a bear, he needs the potion." She put her hand on Basil's arm. "But what about your brother?"

Basil gestured toward the people in the garden. "Her magic broke. The curse should have lifted too. If not, I have the apples and will be able to get him to a healer in time." He pulled away from her and started towards the forest, then glanced over his shoulder. "I'll walk you to the door."

Heather waved goodbye to the ex-servants, who had already broken into Circe's wine. They let out a cheer, thanking her again, and she jogged after the faun.

In a matter of minutes, they were back at the ancient door in the tree.

Heather held the magic staff out to Basil. "You kept your side of the deal. Here's mine."

The faun shook his head and pushed the cane back to her. "You keep it. It's safer with you. Hide it somewhere in your realm so no nasty sorcerers can find it."

She placed the end of the staff on the ground and grasped the handle. "I'll keep it safe."

Basil cleared his throat and cast her an earnest look. "Thank you, Heather. You know, you're a darn good witch."

Heather smiled. Was she a witch? Perhaps she did have magic. Or was it only the staff all along? Did it even matter? The important thing was that they were safe now.

She pulled Basil into a hug. "Thanks for helping me get the potion. And good luck with your brother."

Basil hugged her back. "I'm sure he's okay now, thanks to you."

Heather gave him one last smile and then pushed through the vines. She opened the door and stepped into the dark pine forest of her own realm.

"Carter?" She looked up and down the stone wall and peered through the trees. There was no sign of him. She sighed, hoping he was no longer a bear.

Something pink on the tree stump to the right of the door caught her eye. Her iPod! The device lay on top of the stump. The word "sorry" had been scratched into the wood beside it.

She pocketed the device, and a grin spread over her face. Maybe things would be different now. Maybe Carter would even be nice to her at school tomorrow. Or at least, ignore her.

Whistling, Heather thumped the staff on the ground and started towards home. Consumed with thoughts of magic and new friendships, she didn't notice the white rabbit hopping quietly down the trail behind her.

Even as a young girl, Kandi J Wyatt, had a knack for words. She loved to read them, even if it was on a shampoo bottle! By high school Kandi had learned to put words together on paper to create stories for those she loved. Nowadays, she writes for her kids, whether that's her own five or the hundreds of students she's been lucky to teach. When Kandi's not spinning words to create stories, she's using them to teach students about Spanish, life, and leadership.

Website: http://kandijwyatt.com/

An Unexpected Weapon

By Kandi J Wyatt

On the bus to the high school, rain pelted the windows.

Karlie frowned. "You don't think it'll turn into a bad storm, do you?"

"D-don't worry, i-it can't get too b-bad," Daisy comforted her.

Despite her friend's kind words, Karlie felt the familiar tremor in her hands, and she placed her crooked index finger over her mouth.

"I-it'll be fine."

Karlie wanted to believe Daisy, but the anxious thoughts still plagued her. She fiddled with her phone. Trying to distract herself, she pulled up an image of a shiny, bronze sword, simple in design. Other than its size and the curved pommel reminiscent of Aragorn's weapon in *Lord of the Rings*, there was nothing to say it wasn't a kitchen knife.

"What's that?" Ana glanced over.

"Something I found at Myrtle Beach this weekend."

"A-a sword?" Daisy stared in wonder, her stutter exaggerated with her shock. "Wh-where is it?"

Karlie smiled. This was exactly what she needed to take her thoughts off the storm outside.

"At home, of course! I can't bring it to school, but I want to do some research. You two can help. Here's what it looks like." She showed the other girls another photo, this one taken by the lake where she'd found the weapon. "It's not big—more like a large dagger—but it looks important and old. In the right lighting, it even seems to sparkle. I thought if we looked together, we'd have a better chance of figuring it out."

"D-didn't you th-think to turn it in to the p-police?"

"I wondered about that, but it seemed to have been there for a really long time." Karlie shifted. "Besides, wouldn't it be better to figure out what it is first, instead of bothering the police with a worthless weapon?"

Her friends both nodded.

"This is so exciting. Is the handle metal as well?" Ana leaned in closer for a better view.

"You have good eyes." Karlie squinted at the image, wondering how her friend had figured that out. "It fits my hand nicely as well."

"Look at how shiny it is. Did you clean it up?" Ana flipped her red braids over her shoulders.

"Yep. When I found it, it looked all green and rusty, but then I washed the sand off, and the blade seemed to come to life. It glowed with that brownish sheen. There wasn't a trace of rust anywhere!"

"Really? Th-that's awesome, and st-strange at the same t-time."

"How do we research it?" Ana leaned back.

"Google?" Karlie held up her phone. The others smiled and pulled theirs out, too.

The soft pad of fingers flying over screens was swallowed by their classmates' chatter.

"K-Karlie," Daisy gulped, "are you sure your sword was old?"

"Yeah, why?" Daisy handed her phone over, and Karlie read, then whistled. "That's kind of what this one looked like at first, only it was covered in sand. It had a few pockmarks and even a disfigured section near the point, but when I washed the sand off in the lake, it shone like new."

Ana tapped her finger against her lip. "How can we figure it out? I have a list here of all kinds of swords, but they're based on countries. Any way to know what country this one's from?"

"I'll keep looking." Karlie shrugged. "Thanks for your help."

Ana had been strangely quiet as she bent over her phone. Suddenly she jolted upright. "I've got it!"

"Shh!" Karlie and Daisy said in unison.

"It's Irish. See, these swords here all have that same look to the handle. They have half a circle with an arched triangle at the base. See how the blade meets the grip? It's all one piece." Over the jostle of the bus hitting the speed bump at the high school and the ensuing gathering of supplies and exiting, Karlie couldn't be sure, but it looked right.

"Well, it's a start, but how did an Irish sword make it to Myrtle Beach, Oregon?"

***

After school, Karlie sat on her bed. The wind howled around the house, and rain beat against her window. A quick glance showed the storm had worsened. Her heart raced, and the dreaded heaviness in her chest increased, a feeling she'd not had since moving in with her grandma two months ago. She pushed away the anxiety, reminding herself of what Ana and Daisy had told her: there really wasn't much to fear unless she was out in the ocean during a storm. Yet her mind dredged up the other tales they'd told, of the fierce storms. Would this be one of them?

A notification buzzed, and she pulled up a group message from Ana.

There are four famous ancient Irish swords. It could be one of them. What do you think?

Focusing on the problem at hand instead of the wind outside, Karlie did a quick search on each of the swords. While she was scrolling through the information on Fergus mac Róich, another message pinged.

How would a sword from Ireland end up on the southern Oregon coast?

Daisy's question was more than valid. How *had* the sword gotten to Oregon? Did someone bring it over on a trip? Karlie rejected that idea. When she'd found it, it had looked like it'd been there for centuries.

'Do you think it's magical?'

Two months ago, Karlie would have thought Daisy was crazy.

'Maybe it's from the same place Kajri came from.'

Ana was referring to the unicorn they'd found in Daisy's pasture two months ago.

'Take a look at these. They're all Irish magical swords: Nuada, Aengus, Fergus mac Róich, or the one that belonged to Manannan mac Lir and Lugh.'

The lights flickered, and Karlie cuddled Monster, her cat, forcing her attention to the research instead of her fear.

'Has it ever glowed?' Ana asked. 'If so, it belonged to Nuada.'

Karlie had never seen any light from the sword. She took it out from under her bed and held it up in the air. Nope, no magical glow. No bright light. With a glance around to make sure she had space, she swung the blade. When no sound came from it, she shrugged. At least she'd ruled out Fergus's sword. What good was cleaving the tops off hills anyway? Her phone caught her attention.

'I think I know! Look at Fragarach. It's Manannan mac Lir's sword. He had a horse that could go across water and land, and he could have brought it here.'

'Leave it to Daisy to find a horse.'

'Good job. I'll see what I can find.'

Karlie set to work. The more she read, the more she wondered how she could prove the sword was Fragarach. Her bed shook, and her window rattled. With trembling hands, she slid the blade back under her bed, gathered Monster into her arms and ran to the living room.

"Grandma? Are you okay?" With one arm Karlie hugged the elderly woman.

"Why, of course, dear. Don't worry about the wind. It's just blowing to let us know it's there, and we're alive."

Karlie grimaced. Grandma always had strange sayings, but she loved her anyway.

"Now, why don't I make you up some hot chocolate? That'll help take your mind off the storm."

While Grandma bustled about the kitchen, Karlie pulled Monster close to her, petting his orange fur. He squirmed in her arms but soon settled down to the inevitable. Here with Grandma, the wind didn't seem as fierce, nor her fears as strong.

***

Later that night, Karlie lay in bed with Monster curled up at her side. Alone, the memories of that day a year and a half ago came back full force. It had been an ordinary day of school, cross-country and chores. Without warning, a tornado had set down in her town in California. The devastation had quite literally uprooted her home, leaving her alone and with no place to go.

She turned over, and Monster meowed at her. With loving care, she stroked his soft fur. "I'm glad I didn't lose you, too."

He purred. The wind shook the house, and Karlie squeezed her eyes shut, trying to block it out—along with the unwelcome recollections. It didn't work, even after telling herself that Oregon didn't have tornadoes. She sighed. Maybe more research would take her mind off the storm.

At least it hadn't knocked out cell service. The webpage she'd saved earlier drew her in as she held her phone out in front of her.

Fragarach, also known as The Answerer, The Retaliator and The Whisperer, was made by the Irish gods for Manannan mac Lir and given by him to Lugh, his son. When placed at a man's throat, it forced him to tell the truth, hence The Answerer. The sword could slice through any armour and deliver a fatal blow. No man ever survived a strike from The Retaliator. It was also said to control the winds.

Karlie sat up straight in her bed, dislodging Monster from her stomach. "It could control the wind? I wonder..."

She dropped to her hands and knees and pulled the sword out from under her bed. It gleamed in the light of her reading lamp. The metallic hilt fit into her hand as if designed for her. She tilted her head and listened to the wind. Had it calmed when she picked up the sword? A branch banged against her window. She jerked toward the sound with her left hand up protecting her face and Fragarach pointed at the window. Her elbows remained glued to her side, while her heart pounded as if ready to leap from her chest. *The contents of her old room hurtled around her as she huddled in her closet during the tornado.* She wiped her hand across her face and took a deep breath as the scene shifted back to the safety of her room at Grandma's place.

"It's nothing," she whispered.

Monster looked up at her with wide eyes, as if to ask why she wasn't talking to him, and she collapsed back onto the bed beside him, allowing the point of the sword to drop to the floor. Since it slid further down than she'd expected, Karlie pulled on it. It wouldn't budge. Getting a better grip, she yanked and stared at her carpet. How would she explain *that* to her grandma? Where the sword had been, a hole the exact size and shape of the blade cut through her blue carpet. She lifted the sword back up and laid it gently on the bed as she knelt down to examine the furrow in her floor. The tear was clean, and pink insulation shimmered in the dim light.

A sibilant sound brought her attention back to the bed, where her cat was sniffing the blade.

"Monster, no!" Karlie scooped her cat up before he could cut his nose on the metal.

If this weapon could damage her floor, then she didn't want to see what it could do to Monster. She pushed the sword back under her bed, where it couldn't do any harm and Monster wouldn't bother it. Then she curled up under the blankets again, but her mind wouldn't stop racing. Was it possible she had an ancient, mythological sword in her possession? Would there be any way to not get in trouble due to the hole in her floor?

She must have fallen asleep, because the next thing she knew a crash resounded off her walls and cold rushed into her room.

Grandma swung open her bedroom door. "Karlie! Are you okay?"

Eyes wide, Karlie nodded. Glass glittered in the light from the hall, and rain drenched the carpet. A tree branch hung at an odd angle where her window had been.

"Come on out of here. Bring Monster with you. We'll patch the window in the morning."

Feeling stupid that she couldn't do anything more than nod her head, Karlie rose, slid slippers on her feet and walked toward her grandma, dazed. Beside her, the blanket fluttered on her bed, and she turned. *The sword!* Despite the fact that it'd survived thousands of years in the elements, something called to her. She couldn't abandon it. When she'd picked it up earlier, the cool metal had comforted her. Although she couldn't be sure, she thought the wind had died down at least a little when she held it.

"I'll be right there, Grandma." With the shock wearing off, she grabbed the blanket and wrapped it around the blade to protect it and anything it might want to slice.

A loud boom sent Monster scurrying out of the room as the house shook.

"My word! What *is* that?" Grandma called from the hallway.

"Grandma, wait!" Fear coursed through Karlie's body as she scrambled to catch up to the elderly lady. "I can't lose you like I did..."

"Hush, child. It's okay. We'll be fine. Just take a deep breath."

Once in the hallway, Karlie saw what had caused the problem. The ceiling had caved in near the bathroom.

Karlie stood frozen as she stared at the irregular line of wall and the white dust from the drywall. Rapid breaths escaped her parted lips. As if defying her wishes, the house shook with a gust of wind, and another chunk of drywall came crashing down onto the brown carpet.

Terror gripped her, making her limbs useless. The next thing she knew, she was on the floor, curled up in a fetal position with Monster licking her nose and Grandma talking soothingly to her. She unclenched her arms, which had wrapped around the sword, and noted with amazement that the blade hadn't cut through the cloth nor pierced her flesh. With unsteady hands, she sat up, and Monster curled up on her lap.

"Ugh! I hate this!"

"Karlie, hush, dear. This is the first time it's happened in almost two months."

"It shouldn't happen at all!" She felt bad for yelling at Grandma.

"Maybe, but it's only natural. In time they'll be further and further apart."

Karlie bit her tongue to keep back the words that wanted to spill forth. It wasn't Grandma's fault the tornado had destroyed her life and sent her into panic attacks like this. Her feet began to tingle, giving her notice they were waking up. She tried to wiggle her toes.

"When you can, let's move into the living room." Grandma straightened up. "I'll need to go see if there's anything I can do tonight to keep the rain out of the house. A window was bad enough, but from the sound of it, the rain'll do irreparable damage to the roof and walls."

Inwardly Karlie screamed the word *no*, but outwardly she nodded. There was no way she would let her grandma go out in this storm alone, yet there was no way she could walk out into a storm without another attack paralyzing her. She felt helpless, and a single tear traced its way down her cheek.

Her phone buzzed in her pocket. Withdrawing it, she saw the profile of Daisy's horse, Ginger, and smiled. The one good thing to have come from the tornado was her friendship with Daisy and Ana.

How are you doing? Is it really windy up there?

Had another stupid attack. Two holes in the wall from trees. Grandma wants to go out and check it.

She crossed her fingers that the text would go through and breathed a bit more freely as she received another message from her friend.

Oh, no! That's not good.

Tell me about it.

"Karlie, how are you?" Grandma rounded the corner with her jacket on.

gtg. She ended her conversation.

"Better. I can get up now." As she pushed herself onto her knees, her hand brushed the sword, and she clutched it to her like a lifeline.

Grandma eyed the blanket, but in typical fashion didn't question it. Karlie had used various security items before during storms.

"Do you want a snack before I go check the damage?"

Karlie shook her head. There was no way she could eat right now; in fact, her stomach lurched at the thought of food.

"Well, then I'll go take a look."

"Wait, Grandma." Karlie surprised herself with the confidence in her voice. "I'll go with you."

Grandma stared at her. "Are you sure you're all right?"

Karlie laughed. "No, but you can't go outside on your own. What if something happens to you, and I'm left..." Unable to finish the thought let alone speak it out loud, she trailed off. "I'm going with you." She slid her arms into her jacket and zipped it up, feeling as if she was donning armour.

"You don't have to do this, Karlie." Grandma laid a gentle, wrinkled hand on her shoulder.

"I *do* have to. If I don't, I won't be able to live with myself."

With a final nod, Grandma opened the door, and they walked out into the chaos. Trees roared and evergreen needles flew across the yard, along with branches varying in size from her pinky to her arm. Karlie took a deep breath, hugging the blanket-wrapped sword. If it really was Fragarach maybe she could use it to make the wind stop. Besides, it seemed to give her courage, and she could use all the emotional fortitude she could get.

Her hands shook as she stepped out into the mayhem. Glancing around didn't help; instead the heavy pressure in her chest intensified until she could only hear the pounding of her heart. Shaking, she clutched the sword wrapped in a blanket like a teddy bear. She wanted to curl up in a ball and ignore the world, but Grandma needed her. As if to prove her point, a sudden gust of wind pushed the elderly woman to her knees. Forgetting all else, Karlie sprinted to her.

"Grandma!" She couldn't even hear her own voice over the roar of the wind.

Giving up on words, Karlie hauled her grandma to her feet, hands slipping on the wet sleeve. Once she was sure her grip was strong enough to not let the small woman fly away again, she escorted her back to the door.

"Karlie, thank you, but how will we see if something can be done to fix the roof?"

"Can we really do anything right now?"

Grandma shrugged, looked at her feet and then met Karlie's gaze. "We may not be able to fix it now, but I'd feel better if I could keep some of the water out. I can cover the window in your room, but I don't know about the roof."

With a brief jerk of her head, Karlie turned and left, gripping the sword in her right hand. This time she was prepared for the onslaught, but even so, her legs shook.

Grandma's counting on me to do this. I can't fail her.

One look at the debris flying around was enough to send her to her knees, the contents of her meagre dinner spewing on the ground. Wiping her mouth, she gasped for breath.

Grandma needs me. She repeated the words over and over.

Blinking the rain away, she raised her eyes to the roof. Even in the dim light escaping from the windows and the porch, she could see the damage. Two humongous, old-growth trees stretched across the yard and sprawled over the house. The air left her lungs in a whoosh as she took in the damage, and her heart beat rapidly.

Grandma needs me.

The wind snatched at the blanket in her hand, reminding Karlie of the sword underneath. Taking a deep breath, she uncovered the blade and gripped the hilt hoping it would keep her safe. Her heartbeat smoothed out. Rain glistened on the bronze blade, making it sparkle like crystal. Karlie peered at it through the water droplets on her eyelashes. Was it just the rain or was there a crystalline look to the blade? Another gust pushed her about, but instead of fear sending her to her knees, she planted her feet and held the blade up in front of her.

"Fragarach!" She hurled the name into the storm, but couldn't hear a thing.

How could she control the wind? She puzzled over the issue as she stood with trees bending and branches scurrying down the road. In the glow of the flashlight, the blade glittered, as if it was trying to communicate with her. Taking a deep breath, she stretched out her arm, extending the sword. She hoped the rain and darkness would obscure her from her grandma's view. What would Grandma think? She didn't need a crazy granddaughter on top of everything else.

The roar of wind powered toward her, while the trees bowed under the pressure. She had no clue how much more they could take before breaking. One in particular bent double, and a loud crack followed. Karlie scrambled out of the way as the top of the tree came crashing down. The tip landed at her feet.

Enough! Any more and we won't have a house left. The thought sent fear surging through her limbs. She closed her eyes to hide, but the sound remained, reminding her of the power of the wind.

What could she do? She was so insignificant in comparison to the storm. Already, she'd been pushed about and pelted with rain and debris. How could she unlock the power of Fragarach? Nothing online had even hinted at that answer.

Help, please. Another tree crashing was the only response. *No more!*

She chopped at the branch at her feet, frustration welling up inside her, and the forest around her shifted the opposite direction. Water dripped into her eyes. She used the back of her hand to wipe it away. Again, she whipped the blade around, and she discovered that her action made the debris in front of her fly away. Her eyes widened, and her mouth dropped open. She closed it, but not before she received a mouthful of rainwater. Confidence built within her as she slashed and fought the wind, pushing it back away from her yard, her home. To her amazement, it obeyed and redirected itself around her. With sure steps she traced a path around the house, pushing the gale away from their property. When she reached the front yard again, the sound of branches blowing had calmed, but the eerie stillness of the air only held its breath, ready for another onslaught.

Gathering her courage, she retraced her steps, whipping the sword from side to side and sending the wind from its path of destruction. By the time she returned to the front, she saw her grandma outlined in the doorway. The wind had died down a bit, but if Grandma was talking to her, she couldn't hear. Another round would be required to get the wind under control. Grandma's hand waved at her. With a sigh, Karlie lowered the sword behind her back, only to have a gust push her around. She turned away from her grandma and resumed her march.

Each step, although wobbly at first, became stronger and less of a fight—not only with the elements but also with her own fears. The more she faced her terror, the more she realized she could manage it, and in the process she could protect Grandma, Monster and their home. Sure, repairs would be needed, but not another tree would fall on them if she could help it.

After three more rounds, she heard her grandma calling. "Karlie! Karlie, come here!"

Not sure if she should listen, she lowered Fragarach from its defensive position and waited.

"Karlie?"

"Be there in a minute, Grandma." Her words carried through the air, no longer swallowed by the wind and rain.

"You're okay?"

A smile lit up her face, the sword gripped firmly in her hand. "More than okay, Grandma. More than okay."

Jacob John Rundle was born on September 27, 1985, in Galesburg, IL. He attended Knox College, earning a Bachelor's Degree in Russian Language and Literature. He served eight years in the United States Navy as a Nuclear Mechanic. After finishing his time with the Navy, he moved to upstate New York, writing the stories that need to be written, The Destined Series, in which **AUGUR OF SHADOWS**, the first installment, is scheduled to be released by Three Furies Press in August 2020.

Sierra and the Bow of Golden Rays

By Jacob Rundle

1

No one wanted to spend a nice spring day in a dusty old building where touching anything was prohibited. For the last half-hour, Emily—my best friend since before I could remember—had been explaining the entire plan to me.

"We can see this exhibit. I have this strong feeling it'll come in handy." She pointed to a location on the map. Looking over, I saw that she had tapped the room harboring the Greek Pantheon. "A feeling?" I pushed myself out of my seat. "I don't know, Emily."

Emily chased me through the aisle. "What's wrong now, Sierra?" Her squeak alerted me that she had caught onto my indecision. My patience thinned when she got on her obsessions. What didn't help was the glaring spring sun. "What is going on with this weather?"

"Come on, Emily." I rushed off the bus to get into line. I had never been so happy to see the museum before in my life. To change the subject, I pointed out to her the exquisiteness of the Met.

"Look." I pointed towards its grand entryway. Tall crowned structures, sunbathing in the sun's embrace. It stood guard to the world's most prolific collections of art.

Emily bellowed, "Sierra? Why're you ignoring me?"

"Calm down. Let's just get inside. Okay?" A nice soft breeze brushed the trees, making them dance their whimsical dance. The bouncing water fountains muffled the voices of our other classmates. However, I couldn't escape the acrid aroma of burnt rubber from the bus' old, decaying tires. "They need to change those old things."

"Those tires will pop, endangering all of us." Emily mumbled.

I scoffed. "Is this another feeling?"

"Maybe." She looked away, trying to hide her concern. Luckily, she wasn't the best at hiding her emotions from me. There was a feeling that I couldn't ignore.

"People really do love it here," she muttered. I couldn't believe the length of the lines. It was a good thing that our school had purchased our tickets weeks ago.

"Thankfully." Our class bypassed the other schools. The neighboring schools hissed and huffed for they were already here when our bus arrived. The beads of sweat dripping from their faces told me that they had been waiting for a long time.

"Yeah. It isn't just me who loves this place." Emily dragged me to the atrium. While we were moving through the congested halls, she elaborated on her self-guided tour, pointing out every statue and painting she knew. However, it appeared that we seemed to be walking for hours before we found the room in which she wanted to start.

"You did that on purpose, didn't you?" There was no way that Emily of all people would get lost in this place.

Her big, dark hazel eyes stopped me, "I have no idea what you are talking about." She slid a smile at me.

"I knew it." I laughed.

We entered a room lined with beautiful gold carvings and statues of what had to be Apollo—God of the Sun. There wasn't a day that passed by when Emily didn't tell me something about this Greek figure. The energy and presence within the room was undeniable.

"What are these?" I pointed out the golden shields inside a glass case. When my eyes locked on to the insignia, an electric force flowed through my body. The attraction was magnetic.

Emily faced me. "Those are the shields of Apollo."

"Interesting."

"Let's move on, Sierra." A sharp chill emanated from her words. Her charged smile changed into a stone-cold stare. Pushing past some students from a neighbouring district, I grabbed onto her shoulder. "Emily, what is it?"

She halted against a case, avoiding my question. After a few drawn out minutes, she finally broke her silence. "This feeling in the pit of my stomach. Almost feels..."

"Feels like what?" I asked.

Gnawing on her soft lower lip, she cried, "Like a feeling that something is about to happen. Something bad." The fear in her eyes whirled around like a deep, tenacious storm. I, too, began to worry that she was right.

To refocus her thoughts, I asked about some of the other pieces in the room. "What about this one?" A giant gold facial reconstruction of Apollo with a sun symbol on his neck stood adjacent to us. After I'd asked her this question, my attention was pulled in every direction. The reality was that there wasn't a single piece in the room that wasn't tied to him.

"Was Apollo conceited or something?" I mumbled.

She laughed. "Some would say yes."

"How's that?"

Swiftly, she grabbed my hand and led me across the room. "All of these statues here." She pointed around them. "They all were made in his honour. Apollo was thought of as the sun. Each civilization saw the sun as a massive, creative force. The Egyptians had Ra. The Sumerians had Utu. And so forth."

"I guess I don't really get it. You make it sound like he was the most important God of their time?"

"To some he was." Her rise in intonation suggested that a part of her believed the same thing. "Well, I guess he does look kind of hot, right?" I giggled.

Emily didn't find my comment amusing. Instead, she continued the tour by examining the rest of the exhibit. "Here it says that they have a replica of Apollo's bow." She pointed to the passage, leading to another exhibit, with a picture of a wooden bow with gold-feathered ends. The picture sang to me, bringing back the pulsating feeling in my stomach. "Let's see this thing. It's a recurve, not a compound bow like I used when hunting with my dad. It's more like the archery team's bows, but I think this one might have a heavier draw weight."

"Yeah. You won't be disappointed. They used the wood from a real laurel tree to construct it." She jumped and threw her arms into the air. It was nice to see her excited about something again.

I fought to keep my eyes from rolling too far into the back of my head. When Emily got onto a topic that she loved—she went on and on about it.

"Did you know that his love for Daphne turned into a laurel tree. That's why. His people are paying homage to him." More and more she sounded like a follower of Apollo.

I chuckled. "You're that excited about seeing this thing?" Her eyes lit up like fireworks. There was so no stopping her from seeing it. She rushed to the exhibit with the bow, not realizing she had left me.

"Sierra!" Her voice echoed across the room. I couldn't pinpoint her exact location. After several minutes of pacing back and forth, I found her. “Emily, why’d you dart—” My attention was diverted to the bow. Nothing else mattered when it and I were together. The same siren song hummed in my mind. I no longer cared about anything but the bow.

Emily’s abrupt halt jarred me back into reality, “It’s right over—” She stopped dead cold in the centre of the room, losing her grip on her beloved brochure.

“What’s wrong?”

The colour in her face faded, leaving her almost lifeless. I fanned my hand in her face, trying to bring her back. I didn’t know if she was in shock or something worse.

Nothing.

She tilted her head, listening to some ethereal force. “Nothing. Thought I heard something.” She charged through the crowd like a bull out of Hell. It was unlike her to push people out of the way.

“Hey, stop!” The important thing was to make sure no one caught wind of her behaviour.

She stood before the grand bow over which she obsessed. Did she hear the song as well? Was the bow calling to her?

Whispering into her ear, I asked. “What is going on with you?”

“Sierra, something is off. I know it.”

I wrapped my arms around her and was shocked by the coldness of her skin.

“Okay. I believe you. Let’s go outside for some fresh air.” I had to pry her away from the bow. The unease returned to my stomach, turning in all directions.

Upon exiting the room, a brute security guard brushed against us. “Watch it.”

“Excuse you?” I barked.

The only thing that caught my attention was the smug grin on his flat, pimpled face. "Y'all need to vacate the room. It's being closed for maintenance." He shooed us away from the area.

Gladly, I spun away from the Neanderthal-like guard. "Alright. We heard you." His robust aroma lingered in my nostrils.

As we were leaving the room, an ethereal voice whispered into my ear. "Pick it up." Abruptly I stopped at the threshold, looking around for the source of the voice. The unsettling fact was that there wasn't anyone close enough. "Let's go, Emily." Before I had stepped foot out of the room, a shiny coin on the ground grabbed my attention. As I was ready to step past, the voice returned. "Pick it up."

"This is getting really weird." Instead of ignoring the eerie cry, I swiped the coin, noticing that it had a similar face on both sides—Apollo's. "This guy was really full of himself." Leaving the room, I tossed the coin into my jacket pocket.

Emily and I were halfway down the hallway when our ears were bombarded by a thunderous siren.

Ring. Ring. Ring. Ring.

Frantically I covered my ears, hoping the sound would decrease. Wrong. As I looked back over my shoulder, a group of frantic guards flooded the room. "What's going on?"

"We need to go back, Sierra." Emily picked herself off the floor. "The bad feeling is back. And it has something to do with that room."

"Emily, it's lined with guards. There is no way we can get back in there." Out of the corner of my eye, I saw a massive figure scurry down a side hallway. "What the..." The coiling knot in my stomach gave me the impression that he'd done something. "It's time for us to get outside."

As we made our way through the scared crowds of high school students, we saw that a guard had been posted at the entryway. Emily looked back at me in panic. "What the hell is going on?"

"I don't know. But we need to get back to the bus." My fingers swam around my pocket to make sure the coin was still in my possession.

I sighed. "Thank God."

When it was our turn, I prayed the guard wouldn't find it. My hands become clammy. Sweat dripped down my forehead—a clear giveaway. The guard ceased his search and locked eyes with me. "Is there something you should tell me?"

Clearing my throat, I spat the first thing that came to mind, "Excuse me? Me? Of course not."

Emily barged back into the atrium, spitting fire. "Hey, jerk. Why don't you move this along?"

"What'd you say, little girl?"

Instantly, she clenched her fist. Her face burned with a fiery passion. The reddest I've ever seen it. "Alright, ass."

Stepping in between her and the guard was the only way to get us both out. I grabbed her wrist, signaling for her to breathe. "I'm sorry, Sir," she said, simultaneously annoying the Cro-Magnon guard.

The guard sighed. "Alright. Get going. She's clear." He waved us through, and the pressure within my chest lessened, then ceased entirely.

"Sierra, you looked like a ghost in there."

"Yeah. I didn't want to get caught," I said, rummaging through my pocket and frantically searching for the coin. My fingers ran across the indentations of its solar crest. "Here." I slid the coin in between my fingers and pulled it out to show Emily. "This is why."

Her facial expression must've matched my earlier one—frozen, with a hint of terror. Her body began to tremble. A chill ran up my spine. The cheerful banter of our fellow classmates filled the air.

"Sierra, where did you get that?" She hesitantly stepped toward me. I opened my fist, revealing the coin I picked up from the floor.

I cleared my throat. "Right before we left the room. It was on the floor. It… called out to me."

"Called out to you? How?"

The crowds of students brought out my anxiety. Obviously, we needed to discuss this in private. Getting back on the bus was the only thing I could think of. "Let's talk about this on the bus. Okay?"

She nodded in agreement.

***

Before we knew it, we had reached our school bus, expecting to see the driver, Rosie.

"I wonder where she is?" I asked, knocking on the double doors and trying to get into the bus.

Emily cleared her throat. "She's in the museum, eating lunch."

"How do you know?" Emily had been pretty on-point all day with her feelings. Was she psychic or something?

With the bus locked, we decided to sit under a tree across the yard. To enjoy the remainder of the afternoon, I kicked off my shoes. The warmth of the grass soothed the bottoms of my feet. The blades of grass tickled the spaces between my toes. "I love this."

Emily threw her backpack onto the ground and nestled up against one of the tall maple trees. "I… have to agree."

Rays of light struck the coin, casting a unique glow. "I found it when we were playing detectives in the room." A magical tune filled the air. A seductive force ripped my attention from Emily and to the coin's magic.

"Sierra." Her muffled voice fluttered passed my ear. With the spell not weakening, Emily became louder, "Do you hear me!"

Her heightened tone pulled my attention back into reality, "What?"

"Can I touch it?" She threw her hand towards me. Easily, I handed over the coin. As she examined its surfaces, she shrugged her shoulders. "Hmm."

"Get anything?"

"It isn't what it looks like." Emily peered at it as if trying to see through it.

"What do you see?"

"It wants to be a 1963 penny, but the weight is wrong." Then Emily's eyes bulged. "Gold?"

She squeaked, which she hadn't done since grade school. "I see… something. A dark sky with an evil shadow protruding through the clouds, which are filled with darkness and lightning."

"You see a shadow, reaching out from the clouds? Do you get anything else off of the coin?"

"How do you know this, Sierra?" Emily asked.

"When I touched the coin the first time. This image flashed in my head. A man becoming one with the sun, followed by an image of the exact bow from the brochure. You know… The one that's missing."

Put it into the sun again. Allow my touch to embrace my treasure, and you will be rewarded.

"What was that?" I was dumbfounded by the masculine voice echoing in my head.

"Sierra, what's wrong? You're freaking me out."

I shoved the coin in her face again. "You didn't hear that?"

She shook her head, looking at me like I was crazy. I glanced at the coin again.

Allow my touch to embrace my treasure.

I held the coin up to the sun again, and it radiated bright orange and yellow light.

"Sierra, what did you do?" She scooted back and jumped to her feet, gasping.

Her eyes widened pulling my attention back to her, "Emily, what?"

She pointed down to the grass, and I glanced down at the earthly terrain. The coin had transformed into the wooden bow with golden swan feathers on the ends. My heart skipped a beat.

"Apollo's bow!" I screamed. She jumped and covered my mouth.

She pressed her index finger against her lips. "Shhh. You realize that if the authorities see us with the bow, we will be arrested and charged with a felony?"

"I... I can't believe it. Did you see it? The coin... turned into... the bow," my breathing was deep and heavy.

That is my Divine Golden Bow of Rays, child. Protect it. I will need it very soon. Guard it with your life. And one day, you too will need its power. Ask your friend where her journal is. And then tell her that her journal is under her seat on the bus, three seats back from where you both sat. You'll need this bit of knowledge for proof.

"Where's your journal?" I asked.

"What? How did you know I was thinking of it?"

Brushing the leaves from her face, she paced back and forth, fighting her racing thoughts. Not allowing her fear and panic control her.

"Emily, calm down!" I yelled.

She stopped and fell to her knees. "How did you know that?"

I couldn't tell her a voice from the bow had told me. "I guessed."

Don't lie to her. She needs to know the truth, Sierra. It's imperative that she knows what is happening to you. You'll need her in the future.

"I lied. The bow told me."

She craned her neck away. "What? Do you think that I'm that stupid?"

"But I don't..."

Emily went pale again and ran into the bus.

Seconds later, she screamed.

"Emily!" I ran to the bus, not realizing the bow had fallen from my hands.

Stop. Retrieve the bow.

I stopped and ran back for it. Glancing over my shoulder, I saw Rebecca Sue and Tyler Peterson walking in my direction. They both sneered at me. "Hey, Sierra. Nice toy bow." Their laughter filled my ears. Ignoring them, I ran to the bus. Emily stood by the double doors, holding her journal.

"Sierra, am I psychic?"

I chuckled. "Of course not. It's the bow. There's a voice."

She paused for a moment.

"Sierra, what if the man in the vision is... Apollo?"

I sighed. "Apollo doesn't exist."

You dare speak about a God as such? A simple human like yourself...putting thyself on my level...never!

The Sun dimmed. Grey clouds released their thunderous rage. Fury like the skies had not seen for millennia. The skies' roar would have caused every soul on Earth to shudder. I had nowhere to hide. My life was in *his* hands.

Apollo's.

How dare you speak ill of my divine existence! I can take away what I have given to you if you continue to question thineself. Secure the bow. Tell no one or the consequences will be dire.

"How? They'll see it." It must've looked like I was speaking to myself. Emily was staring at me with a concerned look.

No. They won't. A... toy is what they will see.

"You're talking to yourself." The usual rosy-cheeked complexion still hadn't returned to Emily's face. In disagreement, I pointed at the bow.

"The bow is talking to you?"

"No. It's... Apollo." Racing, imaginable thoughts filled my mind, making it difficult for me to distinguish what was real from what was fake.

I shook my head, "Let's go." I walked towards the bus. I needed to digest the day—especially everything about the bow and Apollo. From this moment on, I had a strong feeling my life was about to change.

2

The next six months were the craziest yet best time of my life, and I owed it all to Apollo. Aunt Daphne came down with pneumonia, and with Apollo's help, she miraculously survived. She despised hospitals her entire life and more so after my Mom passed away. Actually, Aunt Daphne refused to believe in any modern-day medicine. She was always more on the "holistic" side of the spectrum.

I remembered the exact day Aunt Daphne came down sick. It was no question that I would've respected her wishes, however; the doctors told me that she wasn't going to make it—that I needed to contact all of our relatives to prepare for the worse.

Until I thought of Apollo. With deep desperation, I asked him for his divine intervention. I knew that Aunt Daphne would never forgive me for messing with fate by asking a God to rescue her, but it was a chance I was willing to take.

On the morning Apollo visited Aunt Daphne in her hospital room, after five months of long nights, wishing she'd not join Death on his journey into the Underworld, she woke up feeling the best she had ever felt in her life.

Since then, Aunt Daphne was full of life. There wasn't anything she didn't want to do. In my opinion, she was reborn.

This morning was no different, "What time is Emily coming over?" Aunt Daphne poked my stomach with a wooden kitchen spoon, throwing me her newly acquired morning smile.

Looking at my watch, I realized that Emily was late. "Well, she should be here already." A chill ran up my spine.

As soon as the words left my mouth, I regretted saying anything because she would start calling everyone asking where Emily was. Before I could stop her, she left the room to find her phone so that she could call Emily's mother.

Sierra. It's time. Your destiny calls you.

"Thanks, Apollo. For the warning." I sometimes wished he'd show himself instead of speaking to me in my head.

This time I'll be with you. Every step of the way.

A golden light appeared in the living room, filling the house with its brilliance and later, forming into a ball of light. It took shape into a chiselled man, causing my heart to skip a beat. My eyes set their gaze upon him—Apollo, the living embodiment of the Sun.

"I can't do this." Being in his presence scrambled my thoughts and made me stare into his eyes.

"Sierra, the day has come for you to fulfill your destiny." His aura was undeniable.

He stepped closer and brushed his divine hand against my cheek, waking my inner desires. Feelings I never knew I had.

"Are you okay?" He knew the thoughts running through my mind, yet he stayed focused. This wasn't the first time he had dealt with a human.

My jaw was stuck open. No words were said. "Yeah. I'm just... surprised. I mean... You're in my house." My brain slowly processed his presence.

"We don't have much time. She's here. Nyx," he declared in a serious tone.

"Great." All I could do was fight the thoughts racing through my mind. Thoughts of the impending cosmic battle and my possible death. Before I became aware of my destiny, I only imagined what I was going to do tomorrow.

"Haveth the coin, human?" Apollo demanded.

There wasn't a moment that passed when the coin wasn't with me. I wanted to be prepared. "Yes." I patted my shirt pocket.

He nodded.

"I'm waiting for Emily right now."

His silence spoke volumes. Fear and panic began to fill my body. "Somehow, Nyx's minions kidnapped her last night."

My knees gave way, whereas my breathing quickened. Clutching my chest only relieved a small portion of my panic.

"Emily. We must save her. Nyx will not touch a single hair on her head," I cried.

"Nyx's my aunt. An original Titan. Long ago, she was banished because she went mad with loneliness and attempted to destroy everything. Olympus locked her away. Yet somehow she broke free, and now revenge is what she wants."

Images of enormous monsters flooded my mind, stopping me from being able to think straight.

What had I gotten myself into?

For once, I wasn't going to allow my fear to control me. I didn't know how it was going to go. But I was certain I had to try.

"With the help of Emily, you can bring down Nyx. You can weaken her so that I can seal her in a dimensional realm. It isn't a coincidence that you are the one who found the bow. You're a true descendant of mine."

My throat dried, fumbling with only sounds. "Wha...?"

He flashed his devilish smirk at me, causing more unevenness in the pit of my stomach. I couldn't understand anything he was saying. "You're my daughter, Sierra. A demigod."

"A demigod? I don't have any powers though, how can I be a demigod?" I screamed. A sharp pain jabbed the back of my skull and a noticeable lightness in my lower body followed by a sense of dizziness.

"You humans have the wrong idea about demigods. Each one is different. Not every single demigod is going to be Hercules. Some are just 'normal' people. There has to be a balance." His words felt like a divine prophecy.

"I'm one of the normal ones?" I felt like I'd missed out on the destiny lottery with this one.

"You don't have any magical abilities, but you are far from normal. You are the only one who may handle the Sun Bow—my bow. You hold the power to defeat Nyx in your hands."

The fear of Aunt Daphne walking into the living room terrified me. The butterflies in my stomach hadn't settled, my heart was racing, my palms were clammy.

"She won't interrupt us," Apollo declared. Then, he chose to laugh at my nervousness.

"How does all of this involve Emily?" It didn't sit well with me to drag her into this. Besides Aunt Daphne, Emily was my only family.

"Even demigods need help. I always had an oracle. Emily is yours."

"She's an oracle?" She'd kept being right again, over and over. Her feelings. Dreams. It all made sense now.

"We must go. Nyx won't think twice about killing her. She knows what Emily is and wants to terminate the Oracle line."

"Oh, my god. Where is she?" Panic rushed through my body.

Apollo created a sphere of golden energy with an image in its center. I recognized the area. "Central Park. Over yonder," Apollo declared.

I nodded in agreement.

"As you humans love to say—we can go in style," He grabbed my hand and called forth his divine spark. The rays of light shrouded the room and wrapped themselves around us, enveloping us in a sphere of magic. The warmth was bearable, more so than I expected.

"Hold on." We vanished instantly. It was comparable to the movies, traveling through a kaleidoscope of lights. Off in the distance was an enormous, magnificent fortress. I couldn't believe my eyes.

"Is that—?" I pointed my trembling index finger.

He nodded. "Our home—Olympus."

Its divine brilliance was indescribable. Its golden towers reached into the skies with marble statues surrounded by intricately carved columns. Steps led up inside the palace. The place itself emanated pure, holy light.

"I can't believe that's Olympus."

"It's just a domicile for one to slumber, Sierra. Nothing special." He winked.

"Says the God," I responded. The shimmering of the sphere blinded me. Out of reflex, I covered my eyes with my hands. The intensity of light vibrated on the surface of my skin, sending chills all over my body. Sharp nausea developed in my stomach followed by a jolting lifting off the ground, "What is happening?"

Apollo laughed, "Magic."

***

The next thing I knew, we had arrived in Central Park which was shrouded in golden light. There was an eerie chill in the air, leaving my nerves uneasy. The skies were thick with sheets of darkness. The winds howled and whipped through the leafless trees. There was no sign of life anywhere.

"We're in the eye of the storm." The chill of darkness wrapped itself around the trees, making its way across the land and devouring everything in sight.

Apollo shouted over the howling winds. "Call forth the bow. It's needed."

"What about you? What's your weapon?" Apollo's undisturbed stance worried me.

"I'm only allowed to seal Nyx. I'm not allowed to interfere. Mandated by the Fates."

"What—" A funnel cloud roared its way through the city. I brought forth the coin, hoping something magical would happen.

"We've practiced. Now, aim at the centre—her soul." The funnel cloud grew in ferocity, touching the Earth, becoming a massive tornado. Clenching the coin, I called forth for my inner divinity. A light appeared from my chest, surrounding the coin and me. I opened my eyes to see my entire body was wrapped in its embrace. My aura activated the coin's magic, transforming it into my bow.

"Where's the centre?" The flying cars and trees were distracting me, making it difficult to focus. I noticed a certain area that shone brighter—the eye of the tornado.

That's it. Aim at it!

As I retracted the string, an arrow—consisting of pure light—materialized. From Apollo's training, I aimed at the middle section, praying I'd make a direct hit.

Sweat dripped down my face, building up around my closed eye, distracting my focus from Nyx.

Apollo clenched his fist in preparation for the primordial Titaness's appearance. His aura crackled with electrified power. He was no longer a teacher but a battle companion.

A gloomy fog appeared and solidified into shadow demons. Creatures with razor-sharp claws glistened in the deepened darkness. The tornado divided itself into three.

"Sierra, aim at her!" Apollo demanded. He pointed toward the middle twister. The force of the winds picked up. The gusts of wind made it impossible to keep aiming.

"I can't see! It's a tornado!" I cried. The harsh winds blew dust and debris into my eyes. I retracted the string, calling forth another arrow. The middle twister transformed into something—a walking universe.

"Hello, Nyx," Apollo greeted his long-lost relative. Alas, she was hardly amused.

"Son of the Sun, why are you here?" inquired Nyx.

Apollo declared, "To banish you. For the last time."

She chuckled at his feeble words. Releasing a piercing battle cry, she summoned her minions. Lining up in formation, her armies revealed their edge—Emily. Seeing her broke my concentration.

"Emily!"

Encased in darkness. Lifeless in appearance. My instincts told me to proceed. I drew back the string and fired an arrow of light at Emily, praying that she wouldn't be injured. The arrow sliced through the air with precision, thrusting its sharpened edge into the exterior of the shadow.

Piercing through the defences, the arrow released its divine spark inside the shadow. The light eradicated the forces imprisoning Emily, allowing her unconscious body to fall onto the ground.

"No!" Nyx, wanting to regain her prisoner, released a wave of lifeless darkness throughout the land. The tendrils she spawned drilled themselves into the earth and surrounding buildings, devouring everything in sight. Buildings. Plant life. Terrified humans. "I'll enjoy picking the remnants out of my teeth." Signs of life were of no concern to her. Only destruction.

"I'm going to get her," I hissed.

I fought my way through the elevating winds. I wrestled with Nyx's minions, firing arrows at the hordes of demons. However, her armies continued to replenish themselves. A flying tree limb flew into me, knocking me to the ground. My vision blurred and became dark. I slowly opened my eyes. A brute warrior stood a foot away from me. To my surprise, it was the Neanderthal guard from the museum.

"You," I gasped. His stench made me want to heave. He had donned ancient armour plates with chainmail. He must've been their leader.

"I remember you." He chuckled, thrusting his war-beaten sword into the ground.

I gripped the bow. "What're you doing here?"

He sneered. "I'm here for that." He pointed at the bow. Clenching the bow, I scooted away from him.

"Why don't you give it to me? You don't want to hurt your little girly hands." He charged in my direction.

"Little girl, huh?" Rolling away, I had enough room to flip backwards. Gripping the bowstring, I shot an arrow at the guard's head. Flying through the air, the arrow punctured his forehead, and its light eradicated his existence.

"Could a defenceless girl do that?"

I scoured through the debris for Emily. When I found her, her skin was white, frozen in time. The way was clear so I picked myself up and ran to her, dodging more debris along the way.

"Emily." My heart pounded rapidly. She wasn't responding to anything. I glanced around the once beautiful park, trying to figure out how to get her to safety. Tendrils of darkness. Blazing flames. A strong acrid odour, permeating the air, burned my nostrils. All factors to distract me.

Emily was the priority.

I slapped Emily's face, and she became conscious. "Emily, we gotta go."

I wrapped my arms around her. "What's happening?" she mumbled. Using myself as a crutch, I pulled her back to her feet.

"Well, a really old Goddess is trying to destroy the city, and Apollo and I are trying to seal her away again."

"That's it? Then I didn't miss much."

I took a leap and decided to inform her of her own destiny. "Nyx is also after you. Since you're an oracle and all. With your help, we can seal her away." Emily didn't seem surprised by my statement.

"On it." I wrapped her arm around my neck, using my body as a crutch. She was a little heavier than I thought. Avoiding flying debris, we struggled across the battlefield.

"I'll let you know what is about to hit us," I laughed, trying to take her mind off the fact she was in the center of a primordial battle.

"You can do that?" I asked.

She said. "Yes. I had a *feeling* there was something different about me. You just confirmed it."

We made our way back to Apollo. "We need to end this now," I cried.

"Correct," Apollo replied. "You and Emily must come together and weaken her so that I can seal her away. Your divinity and Emily's foresight will save everything."

"Right." I nodded at Emily, who returned the gesture.

Emily closed her eyes with her hands wavering in the air. When she opened them, they glowed with light. "Sierra, call upon your divine light and pierce the source of the darkness's hatred." When the message had been relayed, Emily's eyes returned to their normal hazel.

Still leaning on my shoulder, I sensed Emily was trying to tell me that she had found light. Nyx's armies were destroying everything in their path—poisoning the greenery, demolishing buildings, and feeding off any life in their grasp.

"Let's do this." I drew back the bow, materializing another light arrow.

Use your inner divinity and direct it at Nyx. At her heart.

I looked deep inside myself for what made me special—my divine spark. Images of Apollo and Olympus, as well as a bright light, spread into every cell of my body. The light brought forth my inner strength, accompanied by a golden aura. I continued to draw back the bow, melding it with my power. The arrow grew in size and potency. Bolts of electricity exuded from the rays of light.

Apollo barked, "Sierra, do it!"

I released the bow's string, praying that the arrow hit its mark. The arrow whizzed through the air, eradicating Nyx's armies and her own defences. The arrow pierced her chest, puncturing her darkened heart. The electricity spread throughout her body, paralyzing her and nullifying her magic. She fell out of the sky and on to the ground. She was wide open.

"Apollo, now!"

He projected his golden aura, and it encompassed the entire area. He summoned Olympus's remaining power to seal her away. With a swish of his wrist, a combined beam of power charged its way through the heavens.

The beam pierced the sky and seared Nyx. The combined attacks created a rip in reality, a vortex that pulled her through its threshold. I drew back the bow and shot a second arrow into the pocket dimension, securing her prison.

In the blink of an eye, the mystical veil once again concealed Olympus from mortal eyes.

I exhaled.

"We all can breathe now." Even Apollo released a sigh of relief.

"I... can't believe we did it," I uttered.

"Well, your job is done. Thank you, Sierra."

"What do you mean?" I asked.

"You have fulfilled your task," Apollo said. "And you, Emily—yours has just begun." Emily nodded.

Then, I addressed him. "Are you leaving?"

"Yes. It's my time. Keep the bow. I have a feeling you'll need it again." He stood, staring at us with a cracked half crescent smile across his face. He dematerialized into an orb of light and flew into the sky.

Emily and I stood, looking up into the air.

"You think we will see him again?" I laughed.

"Yes. I do believe so." We headed back to my place to discuss the day we'd had.

Thank you to our Kickstarter supporters:

The Creative Fund
Devon Boddie
Kolyssa VonDeylen
Krista Nims Sundsten
Eileen Bell
Gordhan Rajani
Abiran Raveenthiran
Simon White
Dreaming Robot Press
Ernesto
Anonymous
Cheryl Montgomery
Laurence O'Bryan
Rada Mihalcea
Robert c Flipse
Jessica Walty
Anonymous
Steven Rickett
RP
Jennifer Sundsten
savagediana
Joel Singer
RJHopkinson
Sebastian Sandelin
Naomi Klein
Allison Chaney
I'M A NINJA
Kristie Crawford-Ferguson
Becky Smith
Bernice Mitchell
Mae Harper Sora Duhigg
David Goodwin
Colleen Brown Keenleyside
Stan Matwin
Marvin Hessler
Jan Maksymilian Gronski
Melinda Olson
El Redman
MME
Susan Whitta Brown
Lori Powell
David Bush
Aurora
Michael Fiedler
Dana Tenerife
Guest 1167145874
Anna Kazantseva
Anonymous
Issa Kabeer
Fain Weiss
Marci McCann
Hayley Leadbeater
Jenn Dixon
James Lucas
Jan Maksymilian Gronski
Susan Dunnigan
Stanislaw Szpakowicz
Thomas Bull
Corinne Tessier
Layne Montgomery
Skywings14
Terry J Yuill
Tani Halls
Guy Parent
Kathy Walker
Peggy McAloon
Rupinder
Kaiqua
Jenn Dixon
Rick Greenwood
Simon White
James Lucas

CPSIA information can be obtained
at www.ICGtesting.com
Printed in the USA
BVHW041132040720
582853BV00005B/21

9 781989 092378